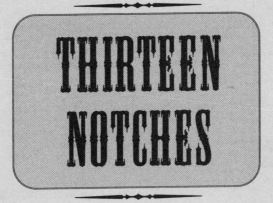

THIRTEEN NOTCHES

HANK EDWARDS

HarperPaperbacks
A Division of HarperCollins*Publishers*

HarperPaperbacks   *A Division of* HarperCollins*Publishers*
        10 East 53rd Street, New York, N.Y. 10022

Cover illustration by Tony Gabriele

First HarperPaperbacks printing: October 1994

Printed in the United States of America

HarperPaperbacks and colophon are trademarks of HarperCollins*Publishers*

❖ 10 9 8 7 6 5 4 3 2 1

1

When U.S. Marshal Sam Benteen stepped out of his adobe house at the edge of the town called Yuma and looked with jaded, steel-cast eyes across the sun-hammered plain to the jagged blue line of mountains dancing on the heat shimmer, he figured this territory had to be the hell spoken of in the Good Book.

Benteen drew a long breath. The air was already hot enough to sear his lungs, and here it was still early in the morning. God, but it was going to be hotter than usual this summer—and the usual was plenty hot enough. A dozen of his forty-six years he had spent in this neck of the woods, and he still wasn't inured to the summer heat. He didn't think he ever would be.

Benteen rubbed his paunch, both satisfied and

a little rueful. His wife Carmelita sure could cook up a fine breakfast. None of that south-of-the-border stuff, either, but a good ol' American breakfast: eggs and pork and sourdough biscuits heavy enough to sink straight to the bottom were you to try to float 'em in a barrel of water. Which, in Benteen's studied opinion, would be a pure-dee waste, since there was nothing finer in the vittles department than Carmelita's sourdough biscuits swimming in butter and wild plum jelly.

Benteen decided those biscuits were his one true weakness. And they were a big part of the reason he was spreading out in the midsection. Yeah, he'd put on a few pounds since getting hitched, and the added weight probably con- tributed to his lack of success in getting used to this hellacious heat, but she had been pretty as a picture, that dusky-skinned gal with the ruby-red lips and big brown eyes and that sinful, sidelong, come-hither way of looking at a man. Still was. Though, like Benteen, she had put on a few pounds. He had never regretted making an hon- est woman of her. He could say as much in his own defense. After forty years of batching it, Benteen had calculated it was time to try his hand at married life.

The one thing he was truly sorry for was the fact that they had not been able to produce any younguns of their own. Now, Carmelita did have a son, Antonio. He was twenty years old. His father had been a *pistolero*. Carmelita said it had happened back in her wild days. She was sorry for everything that had happened back then—everything except Antonio.

Benteen didn't get along all that well with his stepson. He couldn't rightly put his finger on why that was. They just never had hit it off. Too bad, seeing as how they were in the same line of work. Antonio—he went by the last name of Rigas—was one of Yuma's deputy sheriffs. Jack Kyle, the Yuma sheriff, had hired Antonio because he was tough and quick with both fist and gun, and Kyle had wanted a Mexican deputy to help handle the town's considerable Hispanic population.

Antonio was good at what he did. Benteen would give him that much. He didn't walk around anybody, and the local Mexicans feared him, even though some did not respect him, seeing as how he worked for the *gringos*. But Benteen thought Antonio had a deep-running mean streak. It was like the boy had a big chip on his shoulder. Benteen surmised that this attitude had something to do with his pedigree. Maybe it was the bad blood he had inherited from his bandit father.

Six years ago, Antonio had been none too pleased that his mother was marrying a *gringo* lawdog. He still wasn't too happy about it. Benteen and Antonio managed to be curtly civil with each other, for Carmelita's sake, but that was about all.

Benteen sighed. He was a rangy, big-boned man, who had a habit of standing loose and hip-shot. His face was craggy, a map of the hard road he had followed in his lifetime. His nose had been broken twice, and wasn't too pretty to look at. His cold eyes could bore right through you. Though husky, he could move with a fluid grace when in action.

He tugged a suspender strap up onto his shoulder with a blunt-fingered, scarred-knuckled hand—a hand so big it seemed almost to swallow up the bone-handled Colt .45 hogleg he carried on his hip, on the occasions that he had to draw the shooting iron. In his profession, in this country, the occasions came more often than he liked.

A horseman was coming down the street, holding his high-stepping *prieto* stallion to a canter. Benteen knew it was Antonio. He also knew that Antonio wasn't coming to pay a social call. The boy did his best to avoid Benteen, which suited the marshal just fine.

Benteen fished the makings out of a shirt pocket. He fashioned a roll-your-own, clenched it in his teeth, and flicked a thumbnail across the head of a light-anywhere to fire up his quirly. By that time Antonio had arrived in front of the house.

"Are you going up to the prison?" asked Antonio.

Benteen smirked. That was just like Antonio Rigas. No howdy, how the hell are you. The kid wasn't about to waste any of the amenities on his stepfather.

"Why should I?" asked Benteen, being disingenuous just to aggravate the Yuma deputy.

Antonio's smile was sardonic. "You play games

with me. You know what happens today. Frank Allison is getting out."

"Yeah, I know. It's my job to know. Question is, how do *you* know?"

"It is my job, too," replied Antonio, defensive.

"Oh, don't worry. Allison won't hang around in Yuma. Got no reason to."

"It is all they talk about in the *cantinas*."

Benteen shrugged. "Talk is cheap."

"There are a couple of men hanging around town. They look like *gringo pistoleros*."

Benteen took his fourth long drag off the cigarette, then flicked the butt out into the street.

"There are always gonna be gunhawks hoping to make a name for themselves by curling Allison's toes. It's something he'll have to deal with the rest of his days."

"*Sí.* But if they kill him . . ."

"If they kill him, what about the Wells Fargo gold. Ain't that what you were about to say?"

Antonio smiled like a fox. He was a good-looking boy, mused Benteen. Slender and handsome and, they said, a hand with the ladies. He had been blessed with Carmelita's features.

Hearing Antonio's voice, Carmelita emerged from the house, carrying Benteen's duster and hat.

"Antonio!" she said, pleased. "It is good to see you, *mi hijo*."

"*Buenos días, Mamá.*"

"Come inside. I will make you some coffee."

"I cannot. I have business to take care of."

Carmelita nodded, trying to hide her disappointment. Benteen had taken his hat and duster from her and donned them. He gave her a hug and kissed the top of her head.

"See you tonight, little darling."

Anxiety etched itself on her brow. She clung to his arm as he pulled away.

"*Es verdad*, Sam? Is Frank Allison getting out of prison?"

"Reckon it's so."

"Be careful, Sam. He is *muy peligroso*."

"*Hombre malo*," nodded Benteen. He had picked up enough Spanish to get by, without making a conscious effort to do so. The way he figured, this was the United States of America, and if a man didn't know enough English to savvy what Sam Benteen was telling him, well too bad, he'd better make a good guess.

Taking his leave of Carmelita, Benteen started down the road, bending his steps towards the nearby livery where he kept his horse. Antonio wheeled his horse around and rode along with him.

"So what will you do about Allison?" asked the Yuma deputy.

"He served his time."

"*Sí*. But the other man, the one who helped Allison steal the Wells Fargo gold shipment, was never caught. And the gold itself was never recovered."

Benteen stopped in his tracks and squinted up at Antonio, wearing a crooked smile.

"That's it, isn't it? The gold is what you're worried about."

"Twenty-five thousand dollars in gold," said Antonio, and shrugged. "Who would not worry about that much gold?"

"You want to recover it and turn it in."

"There is still a reward offered by Wells Fargo."

Benteen snorted. "Ten percent. Kind of like telling an Apache that if he'll turn in his rifle you'll give him a brand-new slingshot. Show me a man who would turn in twenty-five thousand in gold for twenty-five hundred in greenbacks and I'll show you a tin-plated fool."

"Does that go for you, too, Marshal?"

Benteen shook his head. Antonio never called him Sam—too familiar—or Mr. Benteen, either—too respectful.

"Maybe I'm a fool for being a federal marshal. Sometimes I wonder. But since I am, it's my job to recover stolen property and return it to its rightful owner. Same goes for you, Antonio, in case you were wondering."

Antonio took offense. He was easily offended.

"Are you saying . . . ?"

"Not saying anything more or less than what I said," snapped Benteen. "So just smooth down your hackles. Besides, that gold will never be found. Allison's partner in the road agent business has probably spent it all by now on cheap whiskey and fast women."

"*Puede ser.*"

"No maybes about it. Anybody who's got a notion that Frank Allison will lead them to that gold is wasting his time."

Benteen turned on his heel and headed for the livery. Antonio did not go with him. Instead, the deputy sheriff dug fancy spurs into the flanks of his high-stepping black stallion and galloped back down the street into the center of town, kicking up a plume of pale dust in the process.

The marshal watched him go, shook his head, and put Antonio Rigas out of his mind. Frank Allison, on the other hand, occupied his thoughts at center stage.

Allison was a hardcase, sure enough. Like Carmelita had said, a dangerous man. He had killed thirteen men. All fair fights, but that didn't count for much in Benteen's book. Allison was still a no-account gunhawk turned outlaw, and five years in that hellhole called Yuma Prison would have just made him worse. The frontier wasn't a very safe place to begin with. It was just *less* safe with Allison on the loose.

Still, Benteen couldn't help but feel a little sorry for Allison. First he'd have those young guns to look out for—the ones who would be seeking a reputation by putting him six feet under. Then there were those who defied logic by believing Allison could lead them to that gold shipment.

Reaching the livery, he asked the stable boy to saddle his horse. While he waited, he rolled and smoked another quirly, listening to the clang of the blacksmith's hammer from the forge in the yard back of the livery. When the boy brought up the dun gelding, he asked Benteen if he was going out to the prison.

"They say Frank Allison's getting out today!" exclaimed the bright-eyed younker. "You gonna get into a shoot-out with him, Marshal?"

"I hope not."

"He's the fastest gun of all, you know."

"Is he? You read that in some dime novel, son?"

The boy blushed. "I ain't s'posed to read them things."

"Then don't read 'em. Live by the rules. You break the little ones and you move on to the big ones before long. Then you have to answer to me. I put Frank Allison behind bars, and I can do the same for you if you don't do right. You savvy?"

"Y–yessir," stammered the stable boy, going from crimson to white as a sheet in a heartbeat.

Benteen gave him two bits, tousled his straw-colored hair, and climbed into the three-quarters rig cinched to his dun gelding. It was a relief to be in the saddle. That walk over from the house had got his back to aching again. Benteen shook his head, rueful. He was getting old in a hurry.

The sound of the blacksmith's hammer ringing in his ears, he rode out of town, heading for Yuma Prison.

2

Frank Allison knew what day it was. The guard, Hogel, had kept him informed. So when he heard the big skeleton key scraping in the lock of his cell door, he felt a jolt of excitement run through his lean body. Stretched out on his narrow cot, hands behind his head, he wanted to jump to his feet and rush to the door as it swung open on creaking hinges. But he refrained, mercilessly beating back the hope surging within him.

He had fought this same battle every day for five years. Hope had become his mortal enemy— an enemy he dared not give in to. You had to serve your sentence one day at a time. The old convicts had given him this advice at the very beginning. If you didn't do that—if you lived for the day you would walk out of this hellhole a free man—you wouldn't survive.

Angie's letters had made the fight even more difficult. She had written faithfully and regularly, telling him all about the daughter he had never seen. Sarah had been conceived the last time he had been with Angie, only days before his capture by Marshal Sam Benteen.

Angie would always tell him that they were making do up in Gila Bend, where Angie worked as a seamstress, having quit her job as a dance-hall girl. Worst of all, Angie would write that she was waiting for his release, and sometimes she would let herself speculate about the life they would have together, since he had made a solemn promise to her that he would hang up his guns and walk the straight and narrow.

It was difficult for Allison to keep from sharing in those dreams. But he tried not to. He had survived five years in the worst prison on the face of the earth. Even now he did not give in to hope. He was afraid that if he started counting on getting out today, something would happen to scotch it up.

So he lay there, unmoving, as the door creaked open. He didn't even open his eyes. And he reminded himself to breathe.

"Frank?"

It was Hogel.

"Yeah."

"Get up."

Allison opened his eyes. The beer-bellied German with the heavily jowled face and piggish eyes filled the doorway. A pistol in a flap holster adorned one hip, a billy-club dangled from his belt on the other. He carried a bundle of neatly folded clothes, which he dropped on top of Allison.

"Hello, Hogel."

"This is the day, Frank. Here are your clothes. Put them on. The varden vants to see you."

Allison sat up, swung long legs off the bed, and stared at the clothes.

"Vat's the matter vit you, Frank? Do you vant to stay here a few more years, or somethink?"

"In a hurry to get rid of me? Got somebody else you want to give my cell to?"

"Yah. Alvays somebody else."

Allison stood up and shed his convict tunic and trousers. He put on his own clothes—gray muslin shirt, black twill trousers. Had some trouble getting his boots on. He had gone barefoot a lot these past five years, in order to make the one pair of cheap shoes he received each year last as long as possible, shoes he needed on the days he worked on the chain gang, breaking rocks. The clothes didn't fit too well anymore. He had to notch up the belt to keep his trousers from slipping down around his knees.

"Looks like I could use some home cooking," he said wryly.

"Don't forget your letters."

"No." Allison took the bundle of dog-eared letters from under the thin straw-tick mattress and put them in a pocket. "Thanks, Hogel. You're always looking out for me. 'Course, it wasn't that way in the beginning."

"Not alvays," conceded Hogel. "But then, you are not the same man vhat came in here five years ago, Frank. You have changed. I tell you something. I thought ve vould have to kill you at first."

"You tried."

Hogel shook his head. "Not really. If I had really tried, I vould have, no question."

Allison's thoughts flew back to the early days of his incarceration. The beatings. The time in "the box." The box had damn near killed him, sure enough. The box had boilerplate sides, so small the poor devil inside had to sit with his knees pulled up against his chest and his neck bowed. Set out in the middle of the yard, directly in the hot sun. Two narrow slits, one inch by eight inches, for ventilation. Not enough, when the temperature in the box got up to about a hundred and fifty degrees Fahrenheit. When that happened there just wasn't enough oxygen. There wasn't anything worse than being unable to move while you suffocated.

Men had died in the box. It was the ultimate punishment. If you tried to escape, or struck a guard, you ended up in the box. Allison had committed both infractions.

Yes, in the beginning he had been a troublemaker. But that had changed. The warden was of the opinion that Allison had been broken. He pointed to Allison as proof that his system of harsh punishments worked. Hogel knew better. He knew it had to do with the letters. All the mail the prisoners received was first perused by the guards. This was prison policy, and it was particularly adhered to in Allison's case because the law was still desirous of clues to the whereabouts of his accomplice in the Wells Fargo holdup, not to mention the location of the stolen gold.

As luck would have it, Frank Allison had been assigned to Hogel's cellblock. So Hogel read his mail. The only mail Allison got came from Angie. And Hogel was convinced that after Allison received the letter informing him that he was a father—six months into his prison term—a change had come over the hardcase. Changed, too, was Hogel's opinion of Allison. It had happened very gradually, of course, but now Hogel almost liked Frank Allison.

"Come on, Frank," said the hefty guard. "The varden is vaiting."

Allison stepped out of the cell and turned to walk along the block, with Hogel behind him. Some of the prisoners in the other cells came up to the small cross-barred windows in their cell doors to say a word or two as he passed by for the last time.

"So long, Frank."

"See you on the outside, hoss."

"Don't spend all that gold till I get there."

Another guard unlocked the steel-plated door at the end of the cellblock to let them out into the yard. The brightness of the sun reflecting off the white hardpack of the yard half-blinded Allison. He squinted up at the towers, silhouetted against a brassy, sun-bleached sky, where the sharpshooters stood with their S carbines.

When Hogel knocked on the door to the warden's office, a gruff voice bade them enter.

Warden William Scully was standing at the window, looking out across the serpentine river in the direction of the distant town of Yuma. The window was barred, and Allison, whose previous visit to this office had been five years ago, realized that Scully was in a sense as much a prisoner here as the convicts who were his wards. Only difference being he had a better view, because Scully lived in the prison, in an apartment above the office, accessible by that odd-looking iron spiral staircase yonder in the corner.

Without turning around, Scully said, "Sit down, Allison."

Allison obeyed. He hoped it would be the last order he had to take from this self-righteous sadist.

Scully was a thin, ascetic-looking man. He wore a black frock coat and a black cravat—clothing that struck Allison as being a little outdated for the 1880's.

Eventually Scully turned from the window and settled into the high-backed chair behind his meticulously neat desk of dark mountain mahogany. All the lines in the warden's face turned downwards. His eyes were coal-black, lifeless as a doll's. They gave Allison an uncomfortable feeling.

Scully picked up a single piece of paper, read its contents, glanced coldly at Allison, then returned to the paper. With his expression looking even more sour than usual he signed the paper, drying the ink of his signature with white sand from a small cobalt-blue bottle, then lifting the paper to blow the sand off onto the floor.

"This is your release, Allison," he said. "You've served your time. Personally, I am of the opinion you should have received a much longer sentence. But such was the decision of the jury. We are a society of laws. Which is something I hope you have learned—though I very much doubt that you have."

Allison wanted to tell Scully he didn't give a rat's ass what the warden thought. But he refrained. Release papers signed or not, he wasn't a free man until he walked out of the gate of Yuma Prison. No point in jeopardizing that, so he swallowed his pride.

Scully stared at him a moment, expecting a response, and appeared disappointed when he didn't get one.

"Mr. Hogel here tells me you are a changed man," said Scully. "I believe Mr. Hogel has had the wool pulled over his eyes. Scum like you never changes, Allison. It's a shame that I must release you to prey on honest, decent folk. But it isn't my doing. I am not to blame for the absurdly short sentence that you received. I take some consolation in knowing that you will be back."

"Thank you," said Allison flatly.

Scully's eyes narrowed. But try as he might, he could detect no sarcasm in Allison's tone of voice.

Opening a desk drawer, he brandished a gun-belt. In the holster was a Remington army revolver. The warden looked with distaste at the thirteen notches in the red-maple grips.

"Thirteen notches," he muttered. "Proud of your killing, aren't you?"

"No," said Allison. "That wasn't it at all."

Scully snorted derisively and tossed the gun-rig to Allison, who caught it deftly.

"The tool of your trade," said the warden.

The gun felt heavy in Allison's hand as he pulled it free of the holster, flipped open the loading gate and spun the cylinder.

"You'll have to buy more ammunition," said Scully. He took a ten-dollar gold piece and two silver dollars from a box and put them on the edge of the desk. "Twelve dollars. I don't like the idea of staking criminals, but those are the rules. I guess it is supposed to keep you from robbing the first person you come across."

The gun wanted cleaning, the holster was stiff and needed to be oiled. With the Remington in his hand, Allison found himself inundated with vivid memories of his life as gunslinger and road agent. Unpleasant memories all. But suddenly the past five years seemed like a long dream from which he was just now awakening.

Scully stood up.

"I'll be looking forward to your return, Allison. Hopefully, you'll stay longer with us next time."

Allison rose. He didn't strap on the gunbelt. Turning to Hogel, he almost thanked the guard. But he thought better of it. He had a hunch it would just make things worse for Hogel.

"Take him to the gate, Mr. Hogel," snapped Scully.

Allison started for the door.

"'There is no peace, saith the Lord, unto the wicked,'" quoted Scully. "Isaiah:22."

Allison didn't turn around. Didn't say anything. He walked out the door, followed by Hogel.

3

Hogel escorted Allison through the gate, shook his hand with a solemn "Good luck." The strap-iron door set into the gate slammed shut. The sound of the bolt and padlock being reaffixed was loud in Allison's ears. He didn't turn around. He stood there, in the blue shadow cast by the prison's grim and towering west wall, at the top of a road that snaked down a sagebrush-covered slope to the river a quarter-mile away. At the river was a ferry. The road proceeded on the other side of the river to the distant town of Yuma, a clutter of 'dobe structures and a scattering of dusty cottonwoods, dancing in the heat shimmer.

He was a free man.

Starting down the road, gunrig draped over a shoulder, he noticed a buggy coming up the steep grade from the river crossing. As the buggy drew near, the driver hauled on the leathers to stop the lathered horse in the traces.

"Pardon me, sir. Are you Frank Allison?"

Allison gave the driver a wary once-over. He was a pale man, and thin, with pinched features and small, soft hands. He wore a derby hat, a brown-and-tan checkered suit, and half-boots. He wasn't armed. There was a carpetbag on the seat beside him. He appeared harmless enough, but he also looked nervous—and that made Allison nervous.

"Who wants to know?" asked Allison.

"Allow me to introduce myself. My name is Jonathan Hornsby. I am a writer for Beadles."

"Beadles? The dime novels?"

"Yes. Perhaps you've read some of my work?"

"I doubt it."

"Ah." Hornsby cleared his throat and adjusted the pince-nez riding the tip of his nose. "Are you going into town?"

"I reckon so," replied Allison. "Seein' as how it's the only place I can walk to and get there alive."

"Of course. Let me offer you a ride."

"Why would you want to do that?"

"Simple courtesy, Mr. Allison. It's hot, and a long walk ... ."

"The real reason."

Hornsby smiled. "Trying to put one over on you is an exercise in futility, isn't it?"

"You didn't just happen along."

"No. I came with the express purpose of meeting with you."

"So what is it you want?"

"I want to write the story of your life."

"So long." Allison started on down the road.

"Mr. Allison . . . !"

Allison didn't turn around.

Hornsby got the buggy turned around with some difficulty, and eventually pulled abreast of the gunfighter.

"Mr. Allison!" exclaimed the prose artist. "At least show me the courtesy of hearing me out."

"You're mighty sold on courtesy. Where are you from, Hornsby?"

"Philadelphia, originally. I reside presently in New York City."

"Explains why you talk funny. Been west of the Mississippi long?"

"Well, no."

"You write about this country and its people but this is the first time you've been out this way."

"Well, yes. Mr. Beadles thought it might be a good idea if I captured some of the local flavor, so to speak. Mr. Allison, I implore you, let me give you a ride into town."

Allison jumped agilely into the buggy as it rolled along.

"Is that it?" asked Hornsby, almost breathless with excitement.

"What?"

"The gun. The gun with the thirteen notches."

"Yeah."

"Have you really killed thirteen men?"

"Yeah," said Allison grimly.

"What's it like to kill a man?"

"I don't recommend it."

"They say you're the fastest draw on the frontier."

Allison shook his head.

"Being fast has very little to do with it."

"As I mentioned earlier, I would very much like to write your life's story."

"No."

"But there's money in it, Mr. Allison. You could make a great deal of money. And it would be honestly come by, too."

Allison looked at him.

Hornsby blanched. "I–I didn't mean anything by that, Mr. Allison. I certainly wouldn't cast aspersions . . . "

"Keep your money."

"We could sell thousands of copies back East. The people there are fascinated by characters like you, Mr. Allison. Jesse and Frank James, Buffalo Bill Cody, Wild Bill Hickok, Ben Langley, Bat Masterson, Belle Starr, Wyatt Earp, Longhaired Jim Courtwright. Such stories are much in demand."

"I'm not interested."

"But why not? You would be quite famous."

"I don't want to be famous," snapped Allison. "I want to be left alone."

"I see," said Hornsby, bitterly disappointed.

They rode along in silence for a spell.

"Look," said Allison, "I reckon you came a long way to be here today. But the man you're after is dead. He died back there behind those stone walls and strap-iron. You got here about five years too late."

"You mean . . . you're going to hang up your guns, Mr. Allison? You're not going back to riding that owlhoot trail?"

"No."

Allison put his gunrig on the buggy seat between them.

No more was said until they reached the river. The ferry was moored on the near bank. A man emerged from a ramshackle cabin. Allison remembered him from five years ago. He was a paunchy, unshaven fellow who didn't look like he'd had a bath since Allison had last seen him. Scratching absently at graybacks under his grime-blackened linsey-woolsey shirt, he cocked his head sideways and squinted at Allison.

"You're Frank Allison, ain't you?"

Allison nodded.

"Ferry's closed," said the man gruffly and turned back for the cabin.

"What do you mean, closed?" queried Hornsby. "I just crossed a half-hour ago."

"A half-hour ago there warn't a gunhawk dallyin' yonder 'crost the river."

Allison peered across the river and saw a man leaning in ne'er-do-well fashion against the thick post to which the ferry's towline was secured. A horse was cropping at the short-grass on the bank behind him. The river was a good two hundred feet wide, so Allison couldn't discern the man's features, shaded by the pulled-down brim of his flat-crowned hat.

"Oh, my goodness," breathed Hornsby.

"So, the ferry's closed," reiterated the ferryman.

"You know that man?" asked Allison.

"No, I don't know him, and I don't want to. I don't want to be caught in the middle of some damned showdown, neither."

"I know him," said Hornsby. "I mean, I saw him at the saloon in Yuma. He's a gunfighter, all right."

"How do you know?" inquired Allison. "Did you ask him?"

"Well, yes, as a matter of fact, I did. He was, uhm, rather hostile."

Still scratching, the ferryman was heading back to his cabin.

"Hey," said Allison.

"Huh?"

"I want to get to Yuma."

"Then you can swim, 'cause I ain't takin' you across."

"If you won't, I'll take myself across."

"I reckon not."

Allison took a deep calming breath. The old reactions were still lurking inside him—in the old days he would have changed the obstinate ferryman's mind with his fists, or at the point of his gun. But those days were over.

"Look," he said, trying his level best to be reasonable, "you and your ferry could become all-of-a-sudden famous if there's some leadslinging."

The ferryman frowned, thinking it over.

"Y'know, I never looked at it that way." He squinted speculatively across the river. "You reckon you can take that feller, Allison?"

"I'll worry about that when I get over there."

The ferryman flashed a yellow grin. "Don't get me wrong, but I'd do a whole lot better was he to cut you down. I mean, this here would be the place that the legendary Frank Allison got gunned down. Folks could come from all over just to ride this here ferry."

Hornsby glanced apprehensively at Allison, expecting the gunfighter to take umbrage. To his amazement, Allison just smiled.

"Well, you never know, do you?" said Allison. "This could be your lucky day—and my last."

"Go ahead. Take the ferry."

Allison turned to Hornsby. "Are you going across?"

"I . . . well, I . . . "

Allison started to climb down out of the buggy.

"No, wait," said the reporter. "I'll . . . I'll cross with you."

Allison settled back on the seat. "Anything for a story. Right, Hornsby?"

"Well, I've never witnessed a real gunfight," replied Hornsby, trying to sound nonchalant to mask his fear, and faring poorly in the endeavor.

The ferryman guided the horse onto the raft, returning to the bank to throw off the mooring line. Allison climbed out of the buggy and tackled the towline. The river was running fast and rough, coming off a stretch of shoals above the crossing. He put his back into it. Five years of busting rocks had put some extra muscle in his arms and shoulders. The thick cable sang in its stanchions as the current pushed the ferry downstream, drawing the towline taut.

The closer they got to the far bank, the more nervous Hornsby became. He couldn't tear his eyes off the man who was leaning so casually against the mooring post. Shifting uncomfortably on the buggy seat, his hand brushed the Remington in Allison's gunrig. The reporter snatched his hand away, as though the weapon had somehow scorched his flesh.

"Uhm, excuse me, Mr. Allison."

"Yeah."

"I wouldn't presume to tell you your business, but, shouldn't you be wearing your gun?"

"No hurry," said Allison, pulling steadily on the cable.

"But that man intends to kill you, doesn't he?"

"I reckon."

"You are awfully calm about it."

"No point in getting all worked up about it. He's not going to gun me down. He wants a reputation, not a noose around his neck. So it's got to be a fair fight."

"You sound confident. Yet, as I recall, that fellow Ford shot Jesse James in the back."

"And he got a reputation, all right—as a coward. I'm betting that *hombre* yonder wants better."

"You're betting your life."

Allison smiled. "Life is cheap out here, Hornsby.

You can risk it just by crossing the Mississippi. This desert can kill you in a dozen different ways. Then you've got blizzards and flash floods. Outlaws and Indians. Stampedes. Bad water. A river crossing like this one. A lot of things can kill you out here."

"Then why in heaven's name would anyone want to live here?" asked Hornsby, with fond memories of city life back East dancing through his thoughts.

Allison shrugged. "Gold. Land. A second chance. If you've got the grit to survive, you can make something of yourself."

"Is that why you came?"

"Reckon so."

"And yet you became an outlaw and landed in prison."

Allison peered at him. "It just kinda happened," he rasped.

Hornsby shut up.

A few minutes later they had reached the other side of the river.

4

The gunslinger who was waiting for them across the river seemed to be attached at the shoulder to the mooring post. He didn't move one iota as the ferry came grinding into the shallows. Frank Allison picked up the coiled mooring line and jumped ashore to secure the ferry. This brought him right up close to the gunslinger. The latter was quick to note that Allison wasn't heeled. That threw him. He waited for Allison to say something, but Allison didn't pay him any attention at all. It was as though he didn't even exist, and this provoked the gunslinger, because being noticed was very important to him.

"You run this ferry?" he asked.

"No. I just borrowed it. If you're headed up to the prison you'll have to take yourself across."

The gunslinger was young, with lank yellow hair and a scraggly goatee. His face was long and narrow. He was thin, narrow-shouldered. His thumbs were hooked behind his belt buckle. He was motionless—with the exception of long fingers nervously drumming against the buckle. His guns were a pair of Colt Lightnings in cross-draw holsters, tied down low.

"I ain't going to the prison," he drawled. "I'm waitin' on somebody to come out."

Finished with the mooring line, Allison turned and looked at the gunslinger.

"Maybe it's me you're waiting for."

The gunslinger's faint smile was insolent. "Maybe so, if you're Frank Allison."

"That's me. Who are you?"

"Name's Cade. Billy Cade."

Allison shook his head. "Never heard of you. Sorry."

"Oh, I reckon folks will know my name soon enough."

"Walk away, Billy Cade."

Cade snickered. "You scared?"

"I know what you're thinking. You think that since I've been five years without handling a gun that gives you the edge. Well, you're wrong. You wouldn't stand a chance."

"Mighty sure of yourself. Where's your gun, Allison? You know, the one with all the notches cut into it. I think it'll look good hangin' on my wall."

"You haven't got a wall, Billy Cade. You haven't got a home, or a friend, or a single prospect. All you've got is your life, and it seems to me you're hell-bent on throwing that away."

Cade's face was flushed with anger. He shoved away from the post. "You don't need to preach to me. Just strap on your iron and say your prayers."

Allison shook his head. "You talk mighty tough."

"I can back it up."

Allison wheeled and boarded the ferry. Hornsby was sitting rigidly in the buggy, gaping at a scene from one of his dime novels come to vivid, frightening life right before his eyes. Allison went to the buggy and retrieved his gunrig. He didn't strap it on. He led the horse in the buggy's traces off the ferry. As he passed Billy Cade he dropped the gunrig at the young shootist's feet.

"You want that gun?" rasped Allison. "You can have the damned thing."

With that he climbed into the buggy. Hornsby just sat there, staring at him, the reins loose in his hands.

"Let's go," said Allison.

"But . . . but . . . "

Exasperated, Allison confiscated the reins.

An astonished Billy Cade stared at the gunrig on the ground. This was a development for which he was utterly unprepared. But he recovered quickly enough to leap forward as Allison began to whip up the horse. The gunslinger grabbed some harness and prevented the horse, and therefore the buggy, from moving.

"You're not going anywhere!" he yelled at Allison. "I'm calling you out."

"Not today. Get out of the way."

"You're a yeller coward. Frank Allison's a yeller coward. Well, I'll be goddamned."

"Probably. Now move."

Billy Cade kept one hand on the harness and drew a pistol with the other.

"You're going to get down out of that buggy and strap on your guns or I'll put a bullet right between your eyes."

Moving slowly, Allison descended from the buggy and picked up his gunrig.

Billy Cade let go of the horse and stepped back a few paces. He waited until Allison had strapped on his gunbelt before holstering the Colt and backstepping some more. His arms were crossed in front of him, with the right hand hovering over the Colt on his left hip and his left hand over the pistol on his right hip. He licked his sneering lips.

"Whenever you're ready," said Cade.

Allison just stood there, looking at the young gunslinger with an expression that mixed pity with contempt.

"Slap leather, damn you!" cried Cade.

"After you."

Billy Cade went for his guns.

A single rifle shot shattered the still heat of the morning. The impact of the bullet hurled Billy Cade forward, knocking him down. He landed flat on his face at Allison's feet. Trying to get up, he clutched at Allison's leg. He coughed and spewed blood. Allison shook loose and stepped back, his face a stony mask. Cade collapsed.

Allison glanced at Hornsby. The horrified reporter was staring at the dead man. Then he fell out of the buggy and, on hands and knees, vomited violently. Allison turned his attention to the lone rider on a tall dun gelding who came down off the riverbank.

Reaching the vicinity of the buggy, Marshal Sam Benteen dismounted, wincing slightly as lancing pain shot through the small of his back. He ground-hitched the gelding and walked up to Allison with his Winchester 44/40 shoulder-racked, sparing the man he had killed a mere glance.

"Hello, Frank."

"Marshal."

Benteen held out his hand. "Give me that charcoal-burner."

Allison surrendered the Remington.

Benteen broke the gun open and checked the cylinder. "Empty. I didn't figure Scully had supplied you with any ca'tridges."

"He's not a very generous man."

"I know. What about this one?" Benteen nodded at Cade. "Did he know?"

"I doubt it."

"Why didn't you tell him?"

Allison shrugged.

"You want to die?"

"I'd rather not."

"Didn't think so. I hear you've got something to live for. Must've been foolish pride kept you from telling this kid your gun was empty."

"It wouldn't have made any difference."

"Maybe he would've loaned you some bullets."

Allison just shook his head. "You don't understand. I'm through with killing."

Benteen's eyes narrowed. "What about self-defense?"

"That's funny."

"What is?"

"Every time I killed a man it was in self-defense. Look where that got me."

"You went to prison on account of that holdup."

Hornsby appeared, walking unsteadily around the buggy. He glanced at the corpse, at Benteen, at the star on Benteen's shirt, then at Benteen's rifle—and put two and two together.

"My God, man," he gasped. "You shot him in the back. And . . . and you're a lawman."

"Yessir, I am. U.S. marshal. Have been my whole life. And the reason I'm still alive is I'm not fool enough to ask a gunhawk like this feller here to please turn around so's I can shoot him in the front, all gentleman-like. Who are you, anyroad?"

"Jonathan Hornsby. I'm a writer."

"He wants to write a book about me," said Allison.

Benteen just shook his head.

"Are you the marshal who captured Mr. Allison?" asked Hornsby.

"Good guess."

"Well, perhaps you would let me . . ."

"No," growled Benteen, with such fervor that Hornsby clamped his mouth shut. The prose artist faded back against the buggy.

"Am I under arrest, Marshal?" asked Allison.

"Aw, hell no. But I'll keep this gun for a spell. At least until I've got you on the next stage out of here."

"I'd like a shave and a bath first."

"We'll see."

"Running me out of town?"

"Nope. Think of me as your bodyguard. I've heard there are a few more two-legged snakes like this one hangin' around Yuma, lookin' to make a name for themselves at your expense."

"Mighty kind of you."

Benteen's smile was as warm as a blue norther.

"Don't take it the wrong way, Allison. I don't much cotton to you or your kind. All I'm trying to do is keep the undertaker from being overworked. That's my job, you know. Keeping the peace." He looked bleakly down at the corpse of Billy Cade. "If I can't keep it, sometimes I can *make* it."

The stage to Gila Bend was due to pass through Yuma sometime that afternoon. "I reckon she'll roll in no sooner than an hour from now," announced the laconic clerk behind the counter at the stage station, "and no later than sundown." That was as specific as he could be.

"How much is the fare to Gila Bend?" asked Allison.

The clerk glanced past Allison at Marshal Benteen. Then he fastened hooded eyes on Allison.

"You're Frank Allison, ain't you?"

"That's right."

Benteen stepped up. "He's served his time, George."

"He also held up one of our stagecoaches, Marshal."

"The one stagecoach he wouldn't rob is the one he buys a fare to ride."

The clerk pursed his lips, thinking it over. "Reckon that makes sense, unless he liked it up there in prison. But I ain't sure the Company would care for it much if they knew Frank Allison was riding the line."

"Then don't tell them, George."

"Fare to Gila Bend is a dollar and two bits."

Allison paid up.

"Stage stops here for twenty minutes," said the clerk, as he wrote out Allison's ticket. "Stops for the night at Adobe Springs. Gets to Gila Bend around midday tomorrow." The clerk wrote out Allison's ticket. "You'll hear ol' Coop, the reinsman, blowin' on his bugle as he rolls into town."

Allison collected his ticket. He and his badge-toting shadow stepped out into the shade of the boardwalk. The sun-hammered street was bustling. A haze of alkaline dust rose up to bleach the blue out of the sky. Hornsby was sitting on the bench in front of the depot, writing feverishly in a notebook. He jumped to his feet as Allison and Benteen emerged.

"If I'm not mistaken," said the prose artist, "there's another Billy Cade across the street."

The other two looked across the way and saw the man to whom Hornsby was referring. He wore a serape, with his gunbelt, riding low on his hips, strapped on outside of it. Lank black hair hung to his shoulders beneath a sweat-stained forage cap. Smoke from the cheroot stuck in his teeth curled around the brim of the cap.

"Know him?" Benteen asked Allison.

"I don't think so."

"Looks like he knows you."

"Maybe because you had my face plastered all over the territory on those wanted posters."

"Yeah," growled Benteen. "Blame it all on me." He glanced at Hornsby, and at the notebook in the writer's grasp. "What are you puttin' down on that paper, pilgrim?"

"I'm writing about the shoot-out at the river crossing."

"Really." Benteen snatched the notebook out of Hornsby's hands and perused the page. "You've got real neat handwriting, Mr. Hornsby. But you've also got a short memory. I shot Billy Cade in the back. Mr. Allison did not shoot him in the front."

Hornsby gulped the lump in his throat, painfully aware that Frank Allison was glaring at him in a distinctly unfriendly manner.

"It's . . . it's called literary license, gentlemen. I do not write for a newspaper, you understand. I sometimes embellish the facts to craft a more entertaining story. It's what the readers have come to expect from a Beadles novel."

"Hornsby," said Allison, through clenched teeth, "you're really stretching my patience thin."

"Please understand, Mr. Allison. I . . . "

"*You* understand something," snapped Allison. "I do not want to see my name in any book. I do not want to keep living the life I led before I went to prison. If you put down there that I killed Billy Cade, I'll have every two-bit gunslinger knocking on my damned door, looking for a reputation by filling me full of lead. Don't you get it?"

A chastened Hornsby nodded sheepishly. "Yes, yes, of course. I'll write instead that Marshal Benteen shot Billy Cade. In the front." He smiled at the federal lawman. "No one would believe a United States Marshal would shoot a man in the back."

"Huh," grunted Benteen, expressing extreme skepticism. "C'mon, Frank. I seem to recall you had a bath and a shave on your list of things to do during your brief stay here in Yuma."

Benteen led the way down the street. Two ladies were coming the other way along the boardwalk. Recognizing Allison, they whispered to each other behind their hands and then crossed the street to avoid passing too close to him. Other folks turned their heads and stared—always from a safe distance. Allison wondered how much of this unwanted attention was due to the fact that Sam Benteen was escorting him around town. Some of it, no doubt. But not all, unfortunately.

Truth was, people remembered. His face was well known. His reputation was notorious. That was bad news for a man who just wanted to be left in peace. Maybe, thought Allison, this was too much to ask. Maybe he was going to pay for his sins the rest of his life. He realized now what a priceless gift anonymity was.

Even the barber recognized him. He lathered up Allison's face and stropped the razor, trying to act casual by babbling to Sam Benteen, who had settled his bulk with a weary sigh of relief onto the bench near the plate-glass window. So Allison was forewarned, and when the barber brought the razor close to his throat, Allison grabbed his wrist, moving so fast that the barber nearly jumped out of his skin.

"I want to make sure of one thing," said Allison.

"Y–yessir?"

"I want to make sure you heard right. I want a shave, not a cut throat."

"If it makes you feel any better, Joe," chuckled Benteen, "I've got his gun; so it's not likely he'd shoot you if you was to nick him."

With a wan smile, the barber went to work. Slowly, carefully, he scraped the stubble of whiskers off Allison's stubborn jaw and lean cheeks. Sweat popped out on his forehead and trickled down into his eyes. He couldn't seem to make his hands stop shaking. All in all, he had a lot of things working against him; but somehow he managed to get the job done without drawing blood. A particularly conspicuous achievement—considering that Hornsby popped in to inform Allison and Benteen that the serape-clad gunhawk had reappeared across the street.

Hornsby clearly expected the U.S. Marshal to do something about the gunslinger who was shadowing them, and he was disappointed when Benteen only glanced through the window to confirm the reporter's information before returning to his perusal of yesterday's newspaper.

"You're not going out there?" queried Hornsby.

"For what?"

"Well . . . I . . . the man is obviously up to no good."

"He hasn't broken the law."

"Yes, that's true, but . . . "

"Look, pilgrim, I don't go digging up trouble. I just handle it when it happens."

Hornsby adjusted the pince-nez on his nose and returned to the boardwalk to resume his vigil.

Benteen shook his head. "Frank, that feller's got a hankerin' to see more blood spilled. I'd advise you to stay clear of him. I have a gut hunch he's more trouble for you than all the gunhawks in the Territory."

His shave finished, Allison moved next door to a bathhouse operated by a family of Chinese immigrants. He had a nice long soak in one of the claw-footed iron tubs. Benteen dragged a chair into the curtained cubicle and sat there with him. After five years, Allison had grown accustomed to a lack of privacy. Benteen was just another guard, as far as he was concerned.

"You're getting all spruced up," observed the marshal. "Have anything to do with that dance-hall girl . . . what was her name?"

"She's not a dancehall girl anymore," said Allison, bristling. "And her name is Angie."

"Smooth down your hackles. Did she write to you while you were in prison?"

"What difference does that make to you?"

Benteen gave him a flinty look. "I want to know what you aim to do."

"I aim to settle down."

"And do what?"

"I don't know yet," confessed Allison. "I'll find something."

Benteen was quiet for a spell. Finally he said, "That business at the river with that Billy Cade feller. Makes me wonder if you're not serious about starting over."

"I am."

Benteen nodded. "Well, then, I wish you the best of luck, Frank."

Allison was startled. "Thanks, Marshal."

They went next to a restaurant down the street, where Allison ordered steak and potatoes and coffee and pie. Hornsby joined them. Benteen just ordered coffee. He watched Allison consume his meal like a man who hadn't eaten in a month of Sundays.

"They didn't feed you very well up at the prison, did they, Mr. Allison?" asked Hornsby.

"What they gave us up there I wouldn't feed a cur dog."

Hornsby liked the sound of that. He took time out from his own meal to jot down Allison's remark in his notebook. Benteen watched him with a scowl on his craggy face.

"What are you aimin' to do, Hornsby?" asked the marshal.

"Do? I don't . . ."

"You're not plannin' to write that book about Allison here, now are you?"

"Well, I . . ."

"You're not thinkin' of maybe catching the stage to Gila Bend?"

"Well, it is a free country," protested Hornsby. "Isn't it?"

Benteen let it drop.

A few minutes later they heard a bugle sound.

"That'll be the stage," said Benteen, rolling a smoke.

In no time at all the coach was trundling down the street past the restaurant. A big, bearded character with a bugle dangling by a strap around his neck was handling the leathers.

Allison got up.

"There's plenty of time," said Benteen.

"Don't want to take any chances."

They headed on down to the stage station. The wait seemed like a short forever to Allison. Finally the burly reinsman appeared to perform his walk-around, checking the fresh team of horses the hostler had secured to the traces, making sure the luggage boot straps were secured, and finally calling the all-aboard. A whiskey drummer presented his ticket and climbed into the coach. It was then that Hornsby produced his own ticket and tried to board.

Benteen grabbed him by the collar.

"You're under arrest, Hornsby."

"Arrest?" squawked the prose artist.

"You've been loiterin' around town all day long. Now I ain't sure, but I'm almost certain there's a local ordinance against that kind of behavior. You'll have to spend the night in jail until I make sure. I think you'll find Sheriff Kyle to be a gracious host."

"But I . . . you can't . . . "

"Sure I can."

"But my luggage . . . "

"Hell, don't fret about your luggage," said the reinsman. "I'll bring back anything that ain't claimed in Gila Bend. How's the little woman, Sam?"

"Fine, Coop. Thanks."

Coop looked at Allison. "You ridin' with me?"

Allison gave him his ticket. The reinsman climbed into the box and threaded the leathers through his fingers. Allison made to board the coach, stopped, then turned to offer his hand to Benteen.

"Thanks, Marshal."

Benteen shook the hand. "Do me a favor, Frank. Stay out of trouble. Don't rob any more stages."

"I won't."

Benteen handed over the Remington and Allison boarded the coach. Coop whipped up the six-horse hitch. The stage rolled on. Benteen watched until it turned a corner out of sight. Then he marched the hapless Hornsby straight to the local jail and turned him over to the Yuma sheriff.

"What's the charge against him?" asked Kyle as he locked Hornsby into one of the strap-iron cells.

"I'll think of one in the morning."

Kyle walked outside with the marshal. "Sam, have you seen Antonio today?"

"This morning. Why you ask?"

Kyle fished a badge out of his shirt pocket. "Found this on my desk a few hours ago, when I come back from having lunch. It's Antonio's. Reckon it means he just up and quit. Got any notion why he'd do such a thing?"

Benteen stared bleakly at the badge, wondering how he was going to tell Carmelita.

"Sam?"

"Yeah," growled Benteen. "I think I know what happened."

"Mind letting me in on it?"

"I have a hunch Antonio's lookin' for gold."

"Prospecting? Antonio?"

"Let that pilgrim out in the morning, Jack. Tell him I've gone to Gila Bend—and I'd better not see hide nor hair of him while I'm there."

"Sure thing," said Kyle, bewildered.

As Benteen headed up the street he noticed the serape-clad gunhawk riding past. The marshal turned and watched. The gunhawk reached the edge of town and then turned south, towards the border.

Gila Bend was north.

Surprised, Benteen grunted, winced as he flexed his back, and then kept walking.

6

The man in the serape and forage cap who had shadowed Allison and Benteen through Yuma called himself Lute Springer. When Benteen saw him ride south, his destination was a border town a day and a half's ride across the malpais. As far as Springer knew, the border town had no name. It was of little consequence, and could be found on few, if any, maps.

Springer needed no map, however, to find his way across the desert. He was well acquainted with the hostile, arid wasteland. He knew what to watch out for: Apaches, sidewinders, and scorpions. The horse-laming cholla. Dying of thirst. There wasn't much chance of that in Springer's case. He knew where to find the water holes. He'd spent quite a few years out on the malpais. First as a soldier. Then as a scout against the Apaches.

And now as an outlaw. There were a lot of dangerous things in the desert, but few were more dangerous than Lute Springer.

He reached his destination without mishap.

The village on the Mexican border was a squalid collection of adobe huts. Pausing at the rim of a dusty rise, Springer scanned the miserable scene before him. A creek with water the color of rust was bordered by a few, scrawny trees. At first he didn't see a living soul. Little wonder—it was hot enough to fry a man's brains in his skull. Springer removed his sweat-soaked forage cap and poured the contents of his canteen—a few ounces of warm brackish water—on his head. He could waste water now. There was water to be had in the village. Not that alky creek yonder, but a good well. That well was the only reason the village had survived.

A rickety *carreta* hove into view down among the 'dobes. It was pulled by two mules. The driver of the two-wheeled cart stopped the mules in front of one of the structures. A pair of men emerged from the adobe, carrying a blanket-wrapped bundle which they deposited with ungentle haste into the *carreta*. Another man appeared in the doorway, a shovel in one hand and a pick in the other. The adobe was the local *cantina*, and the man in the doorway Springer could identify, even at this distance, on account of his size. He was obscenely fat. That was Garcia, the *cantina's* proprietor. Springer knew every saloonkeeper from Yuma to Tucson.

A couple of naked urchins appeared in the

sun-hammered street to observe the goings on. They were, mused Springer, symbolic of the way of life here in this nameless village. The twenty or so Mexican residents survived by catering to the outlaws who used this desolate, forgotten place as a haven. There was no farming to be done. No commerce to speak of. The people were desperately poor.

Women and whiskey—that was what hardcases like Lute Springer wanted when they passed through. It was possible, thought Springer, with a crooked smile, that one or both of those dirty-faced brats were his. He didn't know, and he didn't care.

One of the men returned to the *cantina* to take the pick and shovel from Garcia. Then he and his associate clambered into the back of the *carreta*. The driver whacked the rumps of his mules with the reins. The knobheads moved off reluctantly. Springer kicked his horse into a canter, angling down the slope to intercept them.

The local bone orchard was on his side of the creek, and he reached the turgid stream, and the blessed shade of the stunted cottonwoods and willows, as the *carreta* rolled across the shallows. The driver was more interested in emptying a jug of *pulque* than he was in his surroundings, and so the *carreta* had drawn quite close to Springer before the driver's lazy, half-drunken survey disclosed the longrider's alarming presence.

The driver uttered a slurred "*¡Madre de Dios!*" and hauled back on the leathers. The mules didn't want to stop, now that they had begun to move.

The driver hurled curses at the stubborn creatures, and finally managed to stop them. He and the two *campesinos* in the back of the cart stared warily at Springer.

"Plenty hot today," remarked Springer pleasantly. He spoke their lingo fluently. "Even the devil would sweat on a day like this."

"*Sí,*" nodded the driver. "*Es verdad.*"

"I'd say it's too hot to do anything but sleep or drink. But it looks like you boys have a job to do. Who's that you're planting?"

"No one knows his name, *hombre,*" said the driver. "He did not live long enough for anyone to ask. All I know is, he was a *pistolero.*"

"*Gringo?*"

"No, *señor,*" said one of the men occupying the back of the cart with the dead man.

"Mind if I take a look?" asked Springer. "I know a lot of people."

The driver made a go-ahead gesture.

Springer maneuvered his horse to the rear of the cart. Leaning in the saddle, he lifted an edge of the blanket. The dead man stared up at him, a look of surprise frozen on his face.

He was a Mexican, with a thick mustache, pockmarked cheeks, and a nose that had been broken more than once. An ugly bastard, decided Springer. And the bullet hole in his forehead didn't do anything to improve his looks. Springer lifted the blanket a little more—enough to confirm that the corpse had been stripped. If a man died in this town with no name, he left the world just as he had entered it; what the killer didn't see fit to appropriate, as was his right, the townspeople took for themselves.

Springer let the blanket drop.

"It is too hot to dig a grave," said one of the *campesinos* sitting beside the corpse, the pick laid across his knees. "But it must be done. In this heat, a dead man . . . " He shook his head and pinched his nose.

"Who killed him?"

"Weller kill him. He and this one, they gamble."

"Must've been real high stakes to die for."

"*Sí, señor.* They played for the *mujer*, Maria."

Springer grunted. Maria was probably the prettiest whore in this hellhole of a town. But even so, not worth getting your toes curled for.

"This one, he says Jack Weller cheats," added the other member of the burial detail.

"Oh," said Springer, nodding. "That'll get you killed, sure as rain."

"But he is not so bad," said the *campesino*. "He paid us to bury this *hombre*."

"Yeah," said Springer, switching to English. "He's a real prince, Jack Weller is."

"Are you his friend, *señor*?"

"I know him." Jack Weller didn't have any friends.

"Do not make him angry," warned the driver.

"And do not look too long at Maria when he is there," advised the man with the pick.

Springer laughed. "Don't worry. You won't have to dig another grave today. *Adiós.*"

He wheeled his horse around, crossed the creek, and rode on into the village, straight up to the *cantina*.

Garcia had apparently spotted him coming down off the rise to intercept the *carreta*. The obese *cantina* owner was still standing in the doorway.

"Springer," said Garcia. "You haven't been hanged yet."

"Not yet. Weller inside?"

Garcia nodded, turned, and disappeared inside the *cantina*.

Tethering his horse, Springer took the precaution of removing his Winchester repeating rifle from its saddle boot. This village was a den of thieves.

As he stepped into the dark, cool interior, the outlaw could smell just a trace of powder smoke in the sour air. One of Garcia's women was on her hands and knees, scrubbing blood off the floor. Garcia had the only honest-to-God floor in town, and he didn't like bloodstains on it. The woman paused in her work, brushed lank, greasy hair out of her face, and smiled —leered, really— at Springer. Two of her front teeth were missing. Springer wondered if Garcia had done that. The man was hard on his hired help. There was no one else at present in the *cantina*.

"How 'bout a drink, eh, *hombre*?" asked Garcia, lumbering towards the counter—planks laid across several barrels.

"I want to see Weller first."

Garcia scowled. He gestured at a curtained doorway in the back wall.

"*Gracias*," said Springer, and started that way.

"I would not bother him right now," advised the *cantina* owner.

"I appreciate you looking out for me and all, Garcia," drawled Springer. "I truly do. But I just rode all the tallow off my mustang, across eighty miles of the meanest country in the territory, just to see Weller, and I'm not inclined to wait."

Garcia shrugged—a go-ahead-and-get-your-self-killed shrug.

Springer grinned and passed through the curtained doorway.

The hall was dark, and had a rancid smell to it. Springer heard a woman's voice, soft-spoken, followed by a giggle, issuing from behind a door at the end of the hall. He started for the door, got halfway there, and paused. It might not be smart, he decided, to just walk right up to that door and knock on it. Jack Weller was an unpredictable character.

He was about to call out Weller's name when he heard a low growl—a sound like strange, distant thunder. Something lurked in the shadows up ahead. Springer strained his eyes to pierce the gloom, as icy fingers of dread traced his spine.

A large dog rose from the foot of the door at the end of the hallway. Its massive head was lowered, its bared fangs caught a thread of light and gleamed. It looked more wolf than dog, thought

Springer, and it belonged to Weller. Springer had forgotten all about the mongrel.

The outlaw's hand moved instinctively to the handle of the six-gun at his side. The beast seemed to comprehend this motion, and let loose a snarling bark.

The door opened and a man appeared, aiming a pistol at Springer. Silhouetted against lamp-light from within the room, his features were obscured. All that was immediately evident was his husky build. He was tall, broad in shoulder and chest, his legs slightly horse-warped. But Springer knew who it was.

"It's me, Jack. Lute Springer. Don't shoot. I came to talk, not to die."

7

Jack Weller lowered the gun.

"Seen Allison?" His was a deep, gruff voice.

"Yeah."

"Come on in, then."

Springer took another step, but the wolf-dog growled again, stopping him in his tracks.

"Christ!" breathed Springer, afraid, and exasperated because of it. He was afraid of no man, but this dog was a different story. There was something . . . well, just downright evil about the critter.

Weller chuckled. It was a low huffing sound, similar to a locomotive heard from a distance.

"Dog doesn't much like you, Springer."

"I don't care for him, either."

"Careful. You might hurt his feelings."

"I don't care about his damn feelings," said Springer crossly. "Call off your dog, Jack."

"Y'know, I've seen him kill a man. A greaser, down Matamoros way, who was trying to slip up on me one night and slit my throat. Dog took his face off. Always goes for the face. Wasn't pretty."

"To hell with this," said Springer. "I'll just ride on."

"Down, Dog."

The wolf-dog sat down and began panting. Springer mustered up sufficient nerve to slip past the beast in the narrow hallway. Dog watched him, tongue lolling.

Once inside the room, Springer started breathing again.

"Say hello to Maria," said Weller, as he closed the door.

The woman sat on the bed's straw-tick mattress, legs sprawled in immodest abandon, her cinnamon skin covered by a sheen of perspiration. She was young and fairly attractive, with a lissome figure. Pulse quickening, Springer's gaze roamed; then he caught himself, and looked away from her as Weller moved around from behind him.

The room was small and stifling hot. A single window, with the mesquite-pole shutters closed. The only furniture was the rope-slat bed and a rickety chair. Weller was wearing his pants—his shirt was draped over the back of the chair, along with a pair of saddlebags. Weller lifted the flap of one of the panniers and brandished a cheroot.

"Care for a smoke?"

Springer shook his head.

Weller kicked an empty bottle into a corner

of the room. "I'd offer you some mescal, but it looks like I'm all out." His gaze fell on Maria, and he leered. "Anything else in here you might like, Springer?" He chuckled again.

"I'd like to talk about Allison."

A grim look, filled with hate, flickered across Jack Weller's face—what Springer could see of it. Weller wore a full, bristling black beard. His eyes were deep-set and a cold glacier-blue. He reached out and grabbed Maria by the wrist, jerked her roughly out of the bed, and gave her a spin toward the door.

"Go fetch us a new bottle, darlin'."

Maria retrieved her skirt and camise from the floor and left the room. The rough treatment didn't faze her.

As soon as the door had closed, Weller said, "So you say you saw him."

Springer nodded. "I was in Yuma when they let him out."

"So what I heard was true."

"There was some shooting."

"Allison?" Weller was alarmed.

"Naw. He's still above snakes. But a two-bit gunhawk name of Billy Cade tried to draw down on him. That marshal—Benteen—shot Cade down."

"Sam Benteen," sneered Weller. "That tall-walking sonuvabitch."

"I'm surprised somebody hasn't ventilated him yet."

"There's been plenty to try." Weller sat on the bed, leaning back against the wall and puffing vigorously on the cheroot, filling the room with pungent blue smoke. His muscular chest was covered with a dark, thick matting of black hair. Springer could see that Weller had been "ventilated" a time or two himself. There was a bullet scar on his shoulder, right below the collarbone, and another on his side, just beneath the ribcage. Not to mention the ugly scar across his slab-hard belly. Looked to Springer like somebody had tried to gut Weller with a big knife.

Jack Weller was a notorious hand with pistol or knife, and he could kill with his bare hands, too. He was two hundred pounds of pure brawn and unadulterated meanness. But what made him doubly dangerous was that he was smart. One of the smartest men Springer had ever met. Not book smart—Weller could neither read nor write a lick. But he had outfoxed many a badge-toter and Pinkerton man in his long and sordid career as one of the worst longriders in the Territory. He had even outfoxed ol' Sam Benteen—a man whose name struck fear in the hearts of every horse thief and road agent in these parts.

Springer figured that would be one hell of a match—Sam Benteen and Jack Weller. But he wouldn't bet a single shinplaster on the outcome.

"Isn't Benteen the one who chased you and Allison after the Wells Fargo job?" asked Springer.

"Yeah," growled Weller. "That's why Allison and I got split up. On account of Benteen, so hot on our heels. It was over in San Pedro. We thought we'd shaken him loose. I was holed up in a *cantina,* kinda like this one. Benteen comes in and gives me this." Weller touched the bullet scar on his shoulder. "I was lucky to get away with my life. Allison lit out, too. He had most of the gold. You see, Benteen tracked him from San Pedro. Didn't come after me. Benteen tracked him hard, too. Frank figured he was going to get caught. So he hid the loot. Sure enough, Benteen caught him."

"And you have no idea where he hid the gold?"

Weller smirked. "You think I'd be sitting here in this stinking outhouse of a town if I had all that gold? It's only because that *pistolero* I just killed had a few *pesos* in his pocket that I ain't stone-cold broke. So where's Allison now?"

"Caught the stage for Gila Bend. That was yesterday."

"Gila Bend?" Weller scowled. "That ain't nowhere near where we were when Benteen was after us."

"Then if not for the gold, why would he go there?"

The furrows of a puzzled frown disappeared from Weller's forehead. He snapped his fingers.

"Of course! The woman. Angie."

Springer waited patiently.

"Y'see, there was this calico queen up Gila Bend way that Frank was sweet on."

"Frank Allison?" That didn't fit what Springer had heard of the man—a cold and heartless killer who didn't give a damn about anybody.

"Yeah. Who can figure? So that's where he's headed. I'll be damned. Ol' Frank cares more about seeing some slut than he does about collecting that gold. Well, he *has* been in prison for five years. I guess he figures the gold can wait. But some things can't wait."

"Unless *she's* got the gold."

Weller stared at Springer. The thought had obviously never occurred to him.

"By God, you're a smart one," exclaimed Weller. "That's one of the things I like about you."

"Maybe somehow he got word to her where to find the gold," said Springer. "He's got to figure there are a lot of folks who had it in mind to follow him once he got out of prison, hoping he'd lead them straight to the loot."

"Yeah. He's smart, too. He wouldn't run straight to the gold. You're right about that."

"So what now?"

The door opened and Maria entered, bearing a bottle. Weller bounced to his feet and snatched it out of her hand. Pulling the cork with his teeth, he offered Springer the first drink. Springer accepted the offer and washed down some of the dust of the long trail from Yuma with a generous helping of the liquid bravemaker.

"How about you throwing in with me?" asked Weller.

Springer surrendered the bottle. "Do you need a partner?"

"Going up against Frank Allison? Hell, yes. He's faster than I am."

"Maybe he'd just tell you where the gold was, with no problems."

Weller snorted. "We were never exactly friends. We pulled that job together because we had both planned to do it alone. And why would he want to split the gold with me?"

"Well, he's faster than I am, too."

"Together we stand a chance."

"Maybe."

Weller took a swig of the mescal, gave the bottle back to the serape-clad owlhoot. "Besides," he said, "I know I can trust you."

"How do you figure? I could have gone off after Allison and not come back down here to tell you he was out."

"I had to trust you. I can't show my face in Yuma. It's kinda well known there."

"Yeah. I've seen your likeness on a poster or two."

"Fact is, you *did* come back. That shows I can trust you."

All it really proved, mused Springer, was that he wasn't dumb enough to double-cross Jack Weller. He liked living.

"What's my cut?"

"Half."

"Half of the whole thing?"

"Of course."

"What about Allison?"

Weller grinned like a wolf. Springer understood. He nodded.

"I haven't got anything better to do," he drawled. "So I'll go along."

"Good." Weller turned, scooped Maria up and

gave her a bear hug that left her gasping. "You keep the home fires burning, darlin', 'cause I'll be back with my pockets full of gold. And then you and me, we'll head down to Monterey and try our hand at some high living. What do you say?"

For an answer, Maria curled her arms around his neck and, standing on tiptoe, kissed him, darting her tongue into his mouth and grinding her hips against him.

Laughing, Weller pushed her away. "You're a hellcat, sure enough. We'll have us a hot time when I get back."

Springer glanced at Maria as Weller turned to the chair to retrieve his shirt and saddlebags and gunbelt. He wondered about Jack Weller. Maybe he wasn't so smart after all. Springer knew that if he had his pockets full of gold the last place he would come back to was this town—and the last woman he would trust would be Maria. She would slit your throat and rob you blind, given half a chance.

And, too, Weller was proving himself a poor judge of character, after all, if he was willing to trust Lute Springer. Because Springer was already giving some thought to how he would kill Weller once the gold was found.

8

Frank Allison let the rocking of the coach in its thoroughbraces lull him into half-sleep. For the first time in five years he felt truly relaxed. Walking out of Yuma Prison, he'd been tied up in knots. He hadn't known what to expect, but expected the worst. And something bad had happened, sure enough—the gunslick named Billy Cade.

He wondered about that incident at the ferry. He just couldn't bring himself to resort to the Remington Army. He had this gut feeling that if he used the gun just once he'd start back with the old ways again, and the result would be as before. Locked up in some cell. Or six feet under. He wouldn't have any choice in the matter.

This presented him with a dilemma. There were men out there, men like Billy Cade, who figured they could make a name for themselves by killing him. And they were right. But what they couldn't see were the consequences of that kind of reputation. Allison knew. He was living it. He had ridden right straight down that road to hell.

But what was he to do? He had everything to live for. It was waiting for him, up in Gila Bend. A new beginning. Yet men like Billy Cade would keep coming at him. Sam Benteen wouldn't be there next time to do his killing for him. If he didn't defend himself, he wouldn't have much of a life with his family. But if he turned to the gun . . .

The only option, as far as he could see, was to get as far away from this country as possible. He could pack Angie and little Sarah up and they could go north. There had to be a place where no one knew his face. He could change his name. That would suit him just fine. He wanted nothing more than to be shed of the old life, every vestige of it, like a snake sheds its skin, and the name Frank Allison was part and parcel of that old life.

Yet a man needed a grubstake to start all over in a new place. So Allison thought, too, about the gold.

He could go straight to the place where it was hidden—he knew he would have no difficulty finding it. Twenty-five thousand dollars was quite a grubstake.

But he didn't want to have anything to do with the gold. It too was a part of his old life. He thought that using the stolen gold to start anew would, in a way he could not have explained if asked to do so, poison his new beginning. No, he would just have to find some way to start over without it.

He had refused to tell the authorities where to find the gold. They had tried to get it out of him. Warden Scully had certainly done his worst. There had been deals offered. There had been the many occasions when they'd tried to beat it out of him. Allison hadn't talked. He hadn't fallen for their tricks. Not because he wanted the gold for himself. Had he talked, they would have left him to rot in that stinking prison. He was convinced of that.

Maybe, he thought, I'll write Sam Benteen a letter, once I'm a thousand miles away, and I'll tell him where to find that accursed gold.

As for a grubstake, he would just have to make do. Long as he had Angie beside him, he'd be okay.

Thinking about Angie made him a little nervous. It had been so long. He ached to hold her in his arms. But the idea of meeting his daughter Sarah made him more than nervous. Ironic, that a man who had never truly feared man nor beast was now reduced to a quivering state of apprehension by the prospect of meeting a five-year-old girl.

Never in his wildest dreams, huddled by a lonely campfire on the owlhoot trail, had he ever imagined he would be a father. It was pretty remarkable, in fact, that he had even met a woman like Angie, or that he was here now, on the road to Gila Bend and a second chance. The Bible-thumpers said Jesus loved a sinner. Well, maybe that was so.

And he dozed off, feeling free for the first time, and allowing himself not just to hope but to anticipate a bright future.

A half-day out of Yuma they arrived at a swing station, a sod-roofed adobe with adjacent corral at the base of a rocky bluff, built on the site of a sweetwater spring marked by a clump of dusty cottonwoods. Here they would stop for thirty minutes. The horses would be changed out, and a meal made available. The stationmaster was an old codger named McGee. Coop, the reinsman, blew his trumpet as they rolled in, and that brought McGee busting out of the 'dobe, looking hotter than hell with the lid off.

"Quit that godawful racket!" rasped McGee, so furious that he was dancing a jig in the swirling dust kicked up by the hooves of the team and the wheels of the stagecoach. "Good God A'mighty! That infernal noise could raise the dead."

"Well, it raised you up, you ugly ol' goat," snapped Coop. "You're so old you ought to be dead."

"I ain't so old I couldn't whup you to a thin frazzle. And just who are you to call a person ugly? That's like the pot callin' the kettle black. Mister, you're as ugly as hammered mud."

"I may be ugly, but I don't smell near as bad as you," the reinsman fired back, jumping down out of the box and sticking his face in the station-master's. He sniffed, wrinkled his nose, and snorted. "Lord! You smell as rank as horse sweat, McGee."

"Yeah? Well, you smell like wet buffalo."

"I'd punch you right in the nose, except that you ain't tough enough to take it. Shoot! A good wind would knock you clean out of your boots."

McGee guffawed. "I could take your best punch any day of the week and twice on Sunday. Tough enough? When I yell scat, men start to huntin' a hole to hide in."

Allison stepped down out of the coach. From what he'd heard so far he expected blood to be shed any minute.

McGee spared him a flinty glance.

"That's all you got, Coop? One payin' customer? Well, I shouldn't be too surprised. The way you drive that stage, I reckon you done kilt the rest of your passengers."

"That ain't it at all. I had me a full load, but they smelled your beans and blackstrap about a mile down the road and forced me to stop and let 'em out. Said they was gonna walk all the way back to Yuma rather than eat your pizen."

"Speakin' of pizen, I got me some strychnine, with which it is my intention to season your vittles."

"I've been eating your grub for a couple years now, McGee, and since I'm still standing I don't reckon strychnine could put me under no how."

McGee grunted. The hostler, a young tow-headed man, appeared. McGee gestured at the team in the traces. "Change out them nags, Lemuel, fast as you can. It makes my day to watch this ugly galoot head on up the road. He's about as ugly from the back as he is from the front, but the good part about it is that I know when I see his back he's leavin'."

With that parting shot the wiry graybeard stalked back into the 'dobe.

Coop turned and flashed a grin when he saw the look on Allison's face.

"It ain't what you think, mister. McGee and I have been friends for years. I used to ride shot-gun with him. He put down the leathers for good a couple winters back."

"Friends?" Allison was astonished. "Never would've known."

"McGee, he gets a little crotchety at times. But it's a good thing he's got me to talk to. If he talked that way to anybody else they'd shoot him. I kind of get it out of his system."

They went into the station. Coop advised him to eat. McGee's vittles weren't really all that bad. Allison was ambivalent at first. He had butterflies in his stomach from the prospect of seeing Angie and Sarah, and he didn't think he was hungry—until he tasted McGee's beans and blackstrap. McGee watched him wolf down a big helping.

"Don't I know you from somewheres?" queried the station master.

"No."

"Sure I do. You used to rob stages. You're a road agent, mister."

Allison glanced at Coop.

The jehu nodded. "Yeah. I know who you are. Frank Allison. That's why Sam Benteen saw you aboard."

"Allison," breathed McGee. "I thought you was dead."

"He was in Yuma Prison," said Coop.

"Worse than dead," opined McGee. He turned back to his kitchen and fetched the coffeepot off the White Oak stove. Topping off Allison's cup, he added, "It don't amount to a hill of beans what a man done yesterday, in my book. It's what he does today, and plans for tomorrow, that counts."

"I'm through robbing stages," said Allison.

"Glad to hear it."

The sound of a horse cantering across the hardpack in front of the station captured Allison's attention. He was up and at the window in a heartbeat.

A lone rider—a young Mexican—on a handsome black stallion was talking to the hostler, and as the Mexican spoke he threw a glance towards the station. Saw Allison in the window. Their eyes met. Allison didn't know the man, but it was plain as day that the man knew him. Another gunfighter, looking to make a name for himself?

"Antonio Rigas," muttered Coop, standing behind Allison.

"Who's he?"

"Deputy sheriff in Yuma."

Allison could tell by Coop's tone of voice that the reinsman did not much care for Antonio Rigas. He wondered why, but didn't ask, watching in grim silence as Antonio spurred his horse on up the road in the direction of Gila Bend. The hostler went back to work switching out the teams. Allison returned to his meal. But he'd lost his appetite.

When the hostler came inside, his job done, Coop asked him what the deputy had wanted.

"Wanted to know if I'd seen a man come through from down Yuma way, riding a Bar D sorrel. Said he'd have been in a big hurry. Didn't tell me what he wanted him for. I told him I hadn't seen nobody like that."

Coop grunted. "Bat D? Probably a horse thief. God help him if Antonio catches him."

"Why do you say that?" asked Allison.

"Why? On account of Antonio Rigas is one mean *hombre*, that's why. He likes to hurt people. They say his father was a *bandido*. Must be where Antonio got his mean streak, 'cause his ma is a sweet woman. She's hitched to Sam Benteen now."

"What?"

"It's true. You didn't know? I figured you and Benteen went way back."

"We do. But it wasn't one of those relationships where he'd ask me over for dinner."

Coop chuckled. "No, I guess it wasn't."

Allison spoke no more of Antonio Rigas. But

he knew one thing for a certainty: The Mexican deputy sheriff was not in pursuit of a horse thief.

He was looking for Frank Allison.

Or maybe it was the gold.

9

As they were about to leave the station, two people astride one horse came down the road from Gila Bend. A man and a woman, riding double. That usually meant there had been trouble. As the pair drew closer, the look on the woman's face confirmed this.

It was a very pretty face, with big brown eyes and high cheekbones framed by dark chestnut-colored hair. She wore a dusty brown serge traveling suit. A sleeve had been torn at the shoulder seams. She looked angry and afraid and resigned, all at once.

The man was tall and rail-thin. He wore range clothes, but there was something about him that persuaded Allison at a single glance that he was no ordinary cowboy. Allison couldn't have explained how he knew, but this man was a gunslinger. He'd seen plenty in his time, and here was another. The man's features were angular and sun-dark. His eyes were as cold and compassionless as a snake's.

The bay horse they were riding was lathered from stem to stern. It had been run hard, and looked to be just about bottomed out.

Coop had been doing his walk-around, checking the hitch and the wheels. He went forward to meet the two. Allison stayed near the coach, while McGee stood near the adobe's door, shading his eyes from a blinding afternoon sun that had bleached all the blue out of the sky.

"You folks okay?" queried the reinsman.

The man half-turned his head to speak to the woman behind him. "Get down." Almost as an afterthought he added, "Miss Savage."

She did as he commanded—because it *was* a command, not a request. Coop stepped forward to help her. It occurred to Allison that here, too, was evidence that there was more to these two than met the eye. Usually, a man dismounted first, then helped the woman down.

On solid ground, the woman staggered a bit. Exhaustion tugged at the corners of her mouth and eyes. She brushed a stray tendril of hair from her face and smiled wanly at the reinsman, murmured a thank-you.

"Miss Savage!" exclaimed Coop. "I didn't recognize you at first. What's happened?"

"I . . . "

"There was an accident," said the man, his voice devoid of emotion. He dismounted. "Happened up the road a piece. Miss Savage was going to the mission to visit the Indian children there. She went off on her own this time, even though her brother's told her time and again never to do that. So he sent me after her."

"You work for John Savage?"

The man nodded.

"Don't recall seeing you before," said Coop. "Thought I knew all the Slash S boys."

"I don't get into town much."

Coop stuck out his hand. "Name's Coop. I'm a reinsman for . . . "

"Yes. They call me Sledge."

Allison thought that there was a name that fit like a glove. A hard name for a hard man.

"Seems her horse got snakebit," continued Sledge. "Bolted. Miss Savage was thrown from her buggy. She was out cold when I got to her."

"Good Lord. You're lucky to be alive, Miss Savage."

"Yes," she said. "Lucky."

"Knew this station wasn't far," said Sledge. "So we came this way, hoping to find a stage. Wonder could we get a ride back to Gila Bend. My horse is played out, and it would be much better for Miss Savage. I'm sure Mr. Savage will make good on the fare."

"Don't worry about that," said Coop. "Anything for Mr. Savage."

Apparently, mused Allison, this man John Savage was a big augur in Gila Bend.

"You just tie your cayuse to the back of the

coach," continued Coop, "and you can throw your rig up on the top rack."

Sledge nodded. "Obliged." He took the woman's arm. "Come along, ma'am."

Again, it sounded to Allison more like an order than a suggestion.

"If you'd like to lie down and rest for a spell, Miss Savage," said the reinsman, "we don't have to leave right off."

"I . . ."

Once again Sledge spoke for her. "No thanks. Mr. Savage is very worried about his sister. I'm sure it'd be best if we leave now—the sooner we'll get home."

"Of course."

They approached the coach. Allison opened the door and touched the brim of his hat to the lady. She gave him a long look, and Allison got the impression that she was trying to tell him something without words, but he couldn't fathom it. She climbed into the coach. Then it was Sledge's turn to give Allison a long appraisal. With the woman safely ensconced in the coach, Sledge led his horse to the rear of the coach. Allison saw his chance and got into the coach, sitting on the back bench, opposite the lady.

"Is that what really happened, ma'am?" he asked.

The query caught her by surprise. Valuable seconds were wasted as she hesitated, and then she opened her mouth to speak—only Sledge appeared in the doorway and hauled himself up into the coach to take his seat beside her. Allison settled back and looked out the window. Coop closed and secured the door. McGee walked up from the 'dobe as the jehu climbed into the box.

"Try not to kill 'em all 'fore you get to where you're goin'," said the stationmaster.

"It's just a good thing you aren't still driving, you ol' buzzard," was Coop's retort. "This line would've been shut down long ago."

He whipped up the six-horse hitch. The coach rocked in its leather thoroughbraces as they pulled out of the station yard. Allison glanced at Sledge. The man was peering out his window. Allison slid his gaze across to the woman. She was watching him intensely, waiting.

And she shook her head—an answer to his question.

So Sledge was lying.

A few miles from the station they came across the buggy, off in the gray sagebrush at the side of the road. The horse lay dead in its traces. Buzzards had already gathered, circling in the brass-colored sky. Coop slowed the coach but did not seem inclined to stop. So Allison stuck his head out the window and yelled at him to do so. Coop began to climb the reins.

"What are you doing?" barked Sledge.

"Just thought maybe the lady would like to check her rig—make sure she didn't leave anything behind."

"She didn't."

The stage was stopped—Allison threw the door open and stepped out into the bright heat. He looked up at Coop.

"What's wrong?" asked the reinsman.

"Nothing."

Allison walked on out to the buggy. The horse in the harness had been shot through the head. The buggy was upright on its wheels, and on the floorboards was a small carpetbag. Allison glanced back at the stage. He wondered what Sledge's next move would be. He was aware now that Allison knew he had lied. Allison could picture exactly the way it had happened. Sledge had killed the horse. The lady had put up a fight— hence the torn dress. Allison doubted she had been on her way to a mission to visit Indian children. She had a carpetbag packed. Was she running away from something? Or someone?

Allison retrieved the carpetbag and returned to the stagecoach. He tossed the bag up to Coop. Then he climbed back into the coach and settled back on the bench without a word. The reinsman put the carpetbag on the top rack, threaded the reins through his fingers, and whipped up the team.

Sledge glowered at him for a spell. The lady sat very prim and proper across from Allison, her ankles together, her hands clasped tightly in her lap. She was scared clean through. Scared of Sledge, and something more, besides.

"You don't really want to go back to Gila Bend, do you," said Allison.

She looked up at him sharply.

"Mind your own business," advised Sledge.

"Is he making you go back?" asked Allison.

"I said mind your own business," snarled Sledge.

Allison continued to ignore him, gazing steadily at the woman.

"At least tell me if I'm right or wrong," he said.

"You're right," she said.

Sledge moved, launching himself off the bench, drawing the six-gun from his belt, but aiming to use it to pistol-whip rather than shoot Allison. Allison brought a leg up and got a booted foot in Sledge's midsection, then shoved with all his might, slamming Sledge back into the corner of the coach, which rocked violently on its thoroughbraces. Up in the box, Coop shouted something that was drowned out by the thunder of horses' hooves and the rattle, creak, and clatter of the coach.

Allison moved in, swinging. His rock-hard fist connected with Sledge's chin. At the same time he struck at the wrist of Sledge's gun arm with his other fist, knocking the thumb-buster out of his adversary's grasp. Sledge was plenty tough. He took Allison's best punch and struck right back. The blow caught Allison squarely on the jawbone and sent him reeling. He fell down between the benches. With the copper taste of blood in his mouth, Allison tried to get up before Sledge could pin him down on the floorboards.

But he wasn't quick enough. Sledge's knee came down in his midsection, knocking the wind out of him. Allison took another punch, and another. The blows came raining down. He tried to fend them off with one upraised arm, and reached his free hand up over his head, groping for the door handle. There it was! He pulled it down, and at the same instant brought a knee up into Sledge's back as hard as he could. The impact drove Sledge into the door. With the latch undone, the door flew open. Sledge tried to grab hold of the door frame. Allison gathered up a handful of the man's shirt and shoved. Without a sound, Sledge was gone.

Coop was slowing the stage, climbing the reins and cursing at the horses in the hitch. Allison scrambled to his feet and leaned out the open door. He glanced back down the road first, but the plume of pale dust that the coach left in its wake obscured his vision—he couldn't tell what had become of Sledge. He turned to the box and yelled at Coop not to stop. The reinsman gave him a long over-the-shoulder look—and then whipped the team into road gait.

Allison closed the coach door and sank onto the bench across from the woman. He wiped blood off his chin and looked at her. She was staring at him, expressionless.

"You shouldn't have done that," she said.

"He was taking you back against your will."

"Yes. But . . . you shouldn't have made it your affair, Mr. . . . "

"Allison. Frank Allison."

His name did not seem to mean anything to her. "I'm Rebecca Savage."

"I was just trying to help, ma'am."

"Oh, I realize that, and it isn't that I'm ungrateful. But you've simply made matters worse. And made trouble for yourself."

"What are you running from, Miss Savage?"

She shook her head. "Don't get any more involved than you are now. Please."

"Look," said Allison, exasperated. "I generally try to mind my own business. But I bought into this, and I want to know what to expect."

"Do you think he's dead?"

"Sledge?" Allison shook his head. "I'm not usually that lucky."

"You're a hard man, Mr. Allison."

"So is Sledge."

"Yes, he is. That's why my brother hired him."

"What does your brother do?"

"He owns a ranch. And just about all of Gila Bend, too."

"Is he the one you're running from?"

"In a manner of speaking."

"Just tell me straight out, ma'am."

"All right. Yes. I was trying to run away. I don't like the way my brother conducts his business. He is a cruel, unprincipled man, ruled by avarice, who cares only for himself."

Allison whistled. "You don't like your brother very much."

"I'm ashamed to admit that he *is* my brother," she replied, her eyes flashing. "I've stood by for years and watched him use every underhanded scheme imaginable to ruin his competitors. I saw him ride roughshod over decent people. He resorts to bribery and intimidation to get what he wants. And when those tactics fail, he turns to Sledge."

"So you decided to leave."

"That's not why I left. I ran away because my brother tried to use me to further his own business interests."

"I don't savvy."

She looked down at her hands, clasped so tightly in her lap that the knuckles were white.

"My brother is going to force me to marry a man I don't love. Martin Cabell. He owns a mine— a very productive mine. My brother wants it."

"How does he get it by having you marry this man Cabell?"

"It's obvious, isn't it? Mr. Cabell has no next of kin. If he dies, and I am his wife . . . "

"I see. Well, if it's so obvious, why can't Mr. Cabell see it?"

"Because he's a fool. And . . . and he's in love with me."

"He wants to marry you, even though you don't love him."

She nodded.

"You should have just flat out told him what your brother was planning. That would have solved your problem."

"I can't prove it. Martin thinks John is his friend."

"Well, now you can leave."

"It won't do any good to run. I knew that, but I . . . well, I just couldn't stand it. John will just send Sledge after me again. And Sledge will hunt me down no matter how long it takes." She almost broke down then, but managed to compose herself. When she looked up at him her eyes were brimming with tears. "It's you who must run, Mr. Allison. You mustn't step foot in Gila Bend."

"I'm afraid I have to."

"Sledge will kill you. My brother will let him."

Allison's smile was bleak. "But *I* won't."

10

They arrived in Gila Bend at sundown. The first stars were appearing in the purple sky. The golden lamplight spilling from windows, mingled with the violet shadows of night gathering in the alleyways and darkened doorways, softening the harsh countenance of the desert hamlet.

There was one major street, with several more intersecting, all wide and rutted expanses of dusty hardpack. The main street sported several saloons, a dancehall, and a boardinghouse on the south end; on the north end were the more respectable establishments—a bank and a barber, a doctor's office, a livery, and several mercantiles. In the middle was the jail and sheriff's office. Across the street from that were the stage station and the bank—the latter being the only brick structure in town.

It was at the station that Coop climbed the leathers and brought the stagecoach to a halt. Allison made note of the fact that the reinsman had foregone his customary horn-blowing upon arrival, and concluded that Coop had good instincts. The jehu knew there was trouble on this run, and that maybe the trouble wasn't over yet.

Once the coach was stopped, Coop jumped down out of the box and jerked the door open.

"Gila Bend, folks."

He looked at the gun—Sledge's gun—which still lay on the floorboard, but made no comment.

Rebecca Savage sat rigidly on the bench, looking out the window and across the street at the sheriff's office. Allison followed her gaze. The door to the jail opened, and two men emerged through a flood of amber lamplight. He could distinguish precious little about them in the darkness. But he could tell that Rebecca knew exactly who they were.

"It's not too late," he said.

"Yes it is." She took a deep breath, steeling herself for the unpleasantness that she knew lay ahead. "Don't get any more involved, Mr. Allison. I'll always be grateful for what you tried to do, but don't interfere. And for your own sake, leave Gila Bend."

She got out of the coach and started across the street.

"What about your bag, ma'am?" asked Coop.

She did not seem to hear him, and walked on.

The two men left the boardwalk fronting the

jail and moved to meet her. Allison descended from the coach and stood in the shadows clinging to the front of the stage station, as Coop climbed up top to retrieve the carpetbag. One of the men took Rebecca by the arm and led her back to the sheriff's office. All that Allison could tell about him was that he wore a broadcloth suit and white planter's hat. The other man approached the stage. As he drew near, Coop tossed the carpetbag to him, without warning.

"Here's the lady's possibles, Tom," said the reinsman, belatedly.

The man staggered, caught by surprise. He glared up at Coop. "Where's Sledge?"

"Who?"

"The man who belongs to the horse tied up to the back of your coach," snapped the other.

"Oh. He got off a ways back."

"Got off?"

"Look, Sheriff," sighed Coop. "I just drive the stage. When a passenger wants to get off it ain't my business to ask the why and wherefore."

The lawman was skeptical. "He just got off the stage and didn't take his horse. Is that what you're trying to sell to me, Coop?"

Coop shrugged. "Must've been the sun. Y'know how it is, Sheriff. Folks can get plumb addled if they stay out in the sun too long."

The sheriff looked inside the coach, but failed to see the gun on the floorboards. Then he walked around to the back to untie the horse. That's when he saw Allison, and tensed.

"Who are you?" he asked, peering into the shadows.

"Passing through," said Coop.

"What's your handle?"

"Smith," said the reinsman. "His name's Smith."

"Can't he speak for himself?"

"I can talk," said Allison coldly.

The sheriff stared at him a moment. Then, without another word, he took horse and carpetbag and headed back across the street.

Coop came down off the top rack.

"Smith?" asked Allison.

"First name that came to mind."

"Who was that?"

"The sheriff. Tom Hatch."

"You don't much care for him."

"He's got more bluster than backbone. And he's in John Savage's pocket."

"That was John Savage with him?"

Coop nodded. "What the hell did you do with Sledge, anyroad?"

"Threw him off the stage. He was lying through his teeth. Her horse wasn't snakebit. It was shot through the head. And she wasn't going to visit any mission. She was running away."

"She told you that?"

"Finally. That's when Sledge came at me."

Coop glanced across the street. Sledge's horse was tethered to a hitching post in front of the jail. The Savages and Sheriff Hatch had gone inside.

"How come you didn't stop back there on the road?" asked Allison.

"You told me not to. I wasn't too sure you wouldn't shoot me if I didn't do what you said."

"My shooting days are over."

"Really? Let me ask you a question, Mr. Allison. Is Sledge still above snakes?"

"I don't know. Probably."

"Then I have to say that I seriously doubt your shooting days are over. And I would strongly suggest that you take the lady's advice and get the hell out of Gila Bend, pronto."

"She needs help, Coop."

"It ain't your concern."

Allison frowned. He didn't like turning his back on Rebecca Savage. She was trapped, and with no way out. But what could he accomplish, apart from getting himself killed? And he had Angie and little Sarah to consider. He had a greater responsibility to them than to Rebecca Savage.

He nodded. "Reckon you're right."

"So you'll leave town?"

"Not until I find two people. Maybe you can help. I'm looking for Angie Russell. Do you know her?"

Coop was silent a moment. Then he asked, "What are you looking for her for?"

"We're going to be married."

"Christ," muttered the reinsman.

"What?"

"I . . . I don't know where you can find her," said Coop, and turned away.

Allison grabbed him by the arm. "You know plenty. Tell me."

"No." Coop shook his head emphatically. He was afraid.

His trumpet hung by a strap round his neck. Allison grabbed it and at the same time slammed the reinsman against the cambered side of the stagecoach, placing the trumpet across Coop's throat and pressing. He was scared, too. Something had happened to Angie. When he got scared he got angry, and when Frank Allison was angry he was downright dangerous. He realized he was regressing. This was his old way of doing business. But he had to know . . . .

"Tell me where she is," he rasped.

"She's dead," croaked Coop.

The color drained from Allison's face. He pushed away from Coop, backstepping.

"You're lying," he growled.

"No I ain't. I swear it. She died about two months back. Got a fever and just . . . just died."

"A fever . . . "

"Yeah. I knew her. She worked as a seamstress. She made dresses that Mr. Taylor sold in his store."

"I don't believe you."

"She's dead, Mr. Allison. I'm awful sorry. But you can go up to the cemetery and see for yourself if you don't believe me. Some of the folks hereabouts chipped in to pay for a headstone. They say she used to work as a . . . well, that she was a . . . you know. But she up and quit, and most of the people round here didn't hold her past against her. I'm mighty sorry, Mr. Allison. I . . . "

With a strangled sound of pure anguish, Allison turned blindly away, stumbling over the wreckage of his dreams.

11

When Sam Benteen arrived in Gila Bend he rode straight to the sheriff's office. It was professional courtesy to let a fellow lawman know that he was in town. Not that Tom Hatch was much of a lawman, in Benteen's book.

By Benteen's calculation it was close to midnight when he dismounted in front of the jail and hitched his horse to the tie rail. It had been a long ride from Yuma. His back hurt like hell. He flexed his shoulders and winced. Thought again about retiring, and figured he would do more than just think about it when he came up with a valid idea about what to do with himself once he removed the tin star.

The craggy U.S. Marshal walked into the jail and found Tom Hatch over by a gunrack. The

Gila Bend sheriff was loading up a double-barreled Greener he had just removed from the rack. He looked up sharply as Benteen entered, and Benteen recognized that glimmer in his eyes as fear.

"Hello, Benteen," said Hatch, trying to sound casual, and failing.

"Hatch. Trouble?"

"Yeah. Trouble called Frank Allison."

"Got some coffee on that stove?"

"Help yourself."

Benteen walked over to the stove, found a fairly clean tin cup on a nearby windowsill, and poured himself some java from the enamelware coffeepot. The crank was thick as mud.

"What about Allison?" he asked.

Hatch was at his desk now. He laid the scattergun down, lifted his hat, and ran his fingers through sweat-damp hair.

"Hatch," said Benteen, "you look as nervous as a grasshopper in a chicken coop. Why don't you tell me what's got you wound up tight as an eight-day clock. Maybe I can help."

"You don't think I can handle it?"

Benteen shrugged.

"This is my town, you know," said Hatch, defensive.

"Oh? I thought it was John Savage's town."

"I'm the law here."

"I know Allison. Maybe I can fix it so you don't have to use that scattergun."

"I thought he was locked up in Yuma Prison."

"He was. He got out this morning. In fact, I put him on the stage."

Hatch sank into his chair. "You did what? You could've at least sent me a telegram. Given me some warning."

Benteen crossed the room, put the cup down, and leaned forward, big scarred knuckles planted on the desk.

"Frank Allison did his time."

"Means nothing to me. He's still a dangerous *hombre*."

"What's he done to get you so riled, Hatch?"

"Nothin' yet. But he's getting plenty drunk."

"That makes no sense. He came here . . . "

"I know. For Angie Russell. Coop told me. But Allison didn't know she was dead."

Benteen felt his nape hairs crawling. The world suddenly seemed a much more dangerous place.

"Damn it," he muttered.

"Allison didn't take the news too well. He's over at the Antelope Saloon. Just sittin' there drinking like there's no tomorrow."

For Allison, thought Benteen grimly, there is no tomorrow.

"Everybody's cleared out of there," continued Hatch. "I've seen men get crazy drunk and start shooting. . . . "

"What do you aim to do?"

Hatch had a sour look on his face. "When I signed on this damned job I never figured on having to take down a man like Frank Allison."

"You have to be ready to die every day when you put that star on your shirt."

"I tell you one thing," snapped Hatch. "I ain't fool enough to take him on in a gun duel. If he starts shooting up my town I'll give him both barrels of double-ought in the back. And I won't lose any sleep over it, either."

Benteen straightened up. He didn't try very hard to disguise his contempt for Hatch.

"Before you go backshooting anybody, I'll talk to him."

"Be my guest."

"Stay here."

Benteen left the jailhouse, mounted up, and steered his dun gelding south along the main street. He knew right where the Antelope Saloon was.

As he approached the saloon he saw several groups of men, two or three in each group, standing around. They were watching the saloon from various vantage points, at what they considered to be a discreet distance. Their presence annoyed Benteen. He abruptly steered his horse across the street to one group, gathered in front of the boardinghouse across the street from the Antelope.

"What are you gents doing this fine evening?" he asked.

"Us? Uh, nothing, Marshal."

"Waiting for a killing, I reckon," said Benteen sourly. "Well, there won't be any. So why don't you boys just get on home."

They hesitated. Knowing that the notorious gunslinger Frank Allison was in the Antelope

Saloon, and knowing too that it was no coinci-
dence that a United States Marshal was here, they
thought they had good reason to doubt Benteen's
words. It sure seemed to them like the right recipe
for a killing.

"That wasn't a question, really," said Benteen.
"Now git, or I'll have the whole lot of you thrown
into jail on a vagrancy charge."

They moved off then, with surly reluctance.
Benteen wheeled the dun gelding around and
crossed the street to the saloon. Dismounting, he
tethered the horse and headed for the batwings,
pausing only to glower at a pair of men lurking
near the corner of the saloon.

"Git," he said.

They got.

Benteen entered the saloon.

Allison was sitting at a deal table near the back
of the long, narrow room. The only other occupant
was a barkeep, who was standing behind the brass-
railed mahogany, up against the back bar, trying
to be invisible, and looking about as nervous as a
man could look. Allison had his head down. He
looked up briefly to identify Benteen, then looked
down again. Both of his hands were on the table.
Benteen noticed this right off, and was glad. One
hand was cupped around a shot glass. The other
was grasping a near-empty bottle of Old Overshoe.

Benteen moved to the bar.

"Beer," he said.

The barkeep complied. He was shaking as he
placed the glass in front of Benteen.

An elbow on the mahogany, the marshal blew the foam off and sipped. Then he said, "You can go."

"*He* told me to stay," gulped the apron.

"I'm telling you to go."

The barkeep went around the bar and left the saloon in a hurry, not bothering to remove his whiskey-stained apron.

Benteen carried his beer across the room to Allison's table.

"You've got this town pretty stirred up, Frank."

Allison looked up again. Benteen was shocked. How could a man change so much in one day? Allison's features were drawn, almost haggard. His complexion was ashen. His eyes burned bright, as with a fever.

"Angie's dead," he said, his voice hollow, and he choked on the words.

"I heard. God knows, I'm sorry, Frank."

Allison knocked back a shot of whiskey, poured himself some more, shaking the last drop out of the bottle.

"Mind if I sit down?" asked Benteen.

Allison kicked a chair out. Benteen settled his bulk in it with a sigh of relief.

"What happened to her, Frank?"

"She died."

Benteen shook his head. "Life just kicks you in the guts sometimes, doesn't it? Hell. What are you going to do now?"

"It doesn't matter."

"Seems to me you're forgetting something. A little girl."

Allison stared at him. "I haven't forgotten. She's better off not knowing who I am."

"Do you even know where she is?"

"Wherever she is, she's better off."

Benteen exhaled sharply, exasperated. "You know, I've always wanted a kid and never will have one. And you've got one and don't want it. Figure that out."

Allison didn't say anything.

"So is that it?" asked Benteen. "Giving up, Frank? I thought you were a fighter. When the world tries to roll over you you've got to get back up on your feet and push."

"Don't preach to me."

"You're making a big mistake. There's a sheriff out there with a scattergun who's so shithouse scared he's ready to backshoot you. And there's one mean, smart son of a gun name of Antonio Rigas out there, too, somewhere, hoping you'll lead him to that Wells Fargo gold. Probably a few more hardcases, itching to slap leather with you. So, if you want to go out with guns blazing, I don't think you'll have any problem seein' your wish come true. But that would be a crying shame, Frank, 'cause you've got the best part of your life ahead of you."

Allison hit the table with his fist, so hard that he upset the empty bottle and sloshed whiskey everywhere. The bottle rolled off the end of the table. Benteen caught it before it hit the sawdust-strewn floor.

"The best part of my life is six feet under in the local cemetery," rasped Allison.

Benteen watched Allison warily. He could see that Frank was on the edge. If he went over the edge, then there would indeed be some killing tonight. Benteen considered backing down. He didn't want to push this man over the edge. But he couldn't back down, either. If Frank Allison was going to snap, then he needed to be the one to deal with him. That was his job.

"That's where you're wrong," he said gruffly. "Things happen for a reason, Frank. You and Angie—it wasn't meant to be. You might as well step right up to the fact and look it square in the eye. There's something else waiting for you up the road. Something better."

Allison stood up so fast he overturned his chair. "Better!" he gasped, incredulous and furious at the same time. "Something *better* . . . "

"You lay a hand on that Remington," said Benteen, with an icy calm, "and I'll kill you where you stand. I'd hate to do it, but I would."

"Maybe that would be for the best."

"Yeah. I could make sure you were laid out right next to her. That way, your daughter could visit both her parents' graves."

"You bastard."

Benteen sipped his beer. "You're drunk. Sit down."

Allison sat down.

"At least you knew Angie for a while," said Benteen, his tone softer now. "Count your blessings. You know, those letters of hers are what got you through Yuma Prison alive."

"You know about the letters?"

"Warden Scully told me about them."

"He read them, didn't he? I ought to ride back to Yuma and kill that sonuvabitch."

Benteen's blood ran cold. He knew Frank Allison wasn't the kind for idle talk. He was seeing glimpses of the old Allison tonight, and it worried him plenty.

"You'd end up right back in prison."

"No. I'm not going back there."

Benteen shrugged thick shoulders. Chair legs scraped the floor as he stood up. "Well," he drawled, "I hate to see it end this way. But I reckon the next time I see you it'll be over a gunsight."

"Reckon so."

"So long, Frank."

Allison looked bleakly down into his shot glass.

Benteen struck without warning. He still had the empty bottle in his hand. The bottle smashed as he hit Allison over the head with it. Allison slumped sideways out of his chair, out cold.

Letting out his pent-up breath in a gusty sigh, Benteen picked Allison up and draped him over his shoulder, wincing as his back complained by shooting white-hot pain through his body. He carried Allison outside and laid him across his saddle. Then he turned and said, "Get out here where I can see you, Hatch."

The Gila Bend sheriff emerged from the inky blackness of the alley running alongside the Antelope Saloon, and into the yellow rectangle of light thrown by the saloon's plate glass window. The scattergun was cradled in his arm.

"Is he dead?" asked Hatch, hopeful.

"Not hardly."

"You thinking about putting him in my jail, Marshal?"

"Hell, no. I'm taking him out of here."

"How come you're nursemaiding that killer, Benteen?"

"None of your concern."

"Maybe it's that gold you're after."

Benteen shook his head, gathered up the reins, and led the dun gelding down the street, heading out of town.

When Sheriff Tom Hatch rode up to the Slash S ranch house he found Rebecca Savage sitting on the wide gallery, which ran the full width of the adobe structure. At first he thought she was watching the activity in the corral across an expanse of sunbaked hardpack from the house, over near the barn and bunkhouses. Several cowboys were trying to break a mustang, and raising a lot of dust in doing it.

Hatch glanced that way in time to see the bronc throw one of the hired hands across the corral. The Gila Bend sheriff winced as the cowpoke made his impromptu landing. Hatch was glad he wasn't doing that kind of work anymore. What he saw in the corral yonder made him appreciate the job he had. Of course, last night, faced by the unpleasant and downright perilous prospect of confronting Frank Allison, he had reminisced fondly about his carefree days as one of John Savage's hired hands.

Then it occurred to him that he was *still* Savage's hired hand. That pricked his ego, but he shrugged it off.

As he dismounted in front of the house, he noticed that Rebecca wasn't watching the bronc-busting after all. She was staring off into the heat-shimmering distance, a solemn expression on her face. A very pretty face it was, too, thought Hatch. Yes, Rebecca Savage was a fine figure of a woman.

He walked up to her, touched the brim of his hat.

"Morning, Miss Savage."

She blinked, looked up at him, surprised. So lost was she in her own thoughts that she hadn't even been aware of his arrival. Her smile was forced.

"He's inside," she said, and looked away, in effect dismissing him.

This cold shoulder did more than prick Hatch's ego.

"Hatch!"

The sheriff whirled at the sound of his master's voice.

John Savage had emerged from one of the three sets of doors in front of the rambling house. As usual, he was clad in black broadcloth, white muslin shirt, and Middleton half-boots.

"Get in here," said Savage curtly. "We've been waiting for you."

"I rode out as soon as I got word."

One of the Slash S hands had come into town on some other errand, and dropped by the jailhouse to inform Hatch that the boss wanted to see him at the ranch, *muy pronto*. Hatch didn't know what that other errand was. Savage owned a store and a saloon in Gila Bend. He also held title to several other properties, which he had leased out. Savage liked to run his affairs from the ranch.

Savage turned and went back inside. Hatch spared Rebecca one final glance before crossing the threshold. She had resumed staring off into space.

Hatch stepped into Savage's office. Savage was sitting behind an ornate desk of dark mountain mahogany. The man called Sledge was slumped in a chair across the desk from him. One side of Sledge's face was scraped and bruised—an unsightly mess.

"Morning, Mr. Savage. Sledge."

Sledge just looked at him with cold, hooded eyes. His dark, angular features might have been carved from stone for all the emotion they displayed.

"A man got off the stage from Yuma last night," said Savage. "Who was he?"

Hatch peered at Savage, trying to figure out what he was getting at. John Savage was a medium-size man, with a pale, round face and thinning red hair. His hands were small and white and soft looking. In fact, Savage was a soft-looking man. But he made up for that with ruthless ambition and a hard heart. He wasn't anything like his father.

The Gila Bend sheriff remembered Will Savage. A tough but fair-minded man, Will had put Hatch on the Slash S payroll. Didn't make any sense that someone like Will Savage could sire a son like John.

The younger Savage wasn't much of a hand with either gun or rope. He didn't know much about breaking horses or brushpopping steers. He didn't care to know. He hired men to do his cowboying and bronc-busting and shooting for him. What John Savage *did* want was to own everything and everybody he could get his greedy little hands on—and he was well on his way to doing just that.

"Well?" asked Savage, impatient.

"That was Frank Allison."

Brows raised, Savage glanced at Sledge. "Allison? You tangled with Frank Allison, the gunfighter?"

"Outlaw," corrected Hatch. "Stage holdups and such. He went to Yuma Prison for stealing a Wells Fargo gold shipment five years ago."

"Yes, I remember now. Did they ever find that gold?"

Hatch shook his head.

"Do you know about this man Allison?" Savage asked Sledge.

Sledge shrugged. "Heard the name."

"You heard about him all the way up in Wyoming?" wondered Hatch.

"That's what I said."

Hatch knew that Sledge had come from up north a year ago, where he had worked for a cattlemen's association, tracking down rustlers. They called such men regulators. Just a fancy name for killers. There was no way of knowing how many men Sledge had gunned down, but the association didn't care. All they looked at were results. And from what Hatch had heard, there had been a lot less rustling in those parts after Sledge had spent a couple of winters prowling the northern range.

"They say Allison has killed thirteen men," said Hatch. "All fair gunfights. I'm told he notches his gun, too."

Sledge looked unimpressed. "Where is he now?"

"Gone."

Sledge stood up, and now there was an expression on his face—one that made Hatch's blood run cold.

"What do you mean, gone?"

"Look," said Hatch. "This is what happened. Allison came to Gila Bend looking for a woman named Angie Russell. She died a few months back. The news tore Allison up. He got to drinking heavy. That ran everybody out of the Antelope Saloon. They were afraid he was going to start shooting up the place."

"You weren't afraid, though, were you, Hatch?" smirked Savage.

Hatch became defensive. He didn't like what Savage was implying, not one bit.

"I was ready to do what I had to if he started trouble."

"My," said Savage, his words dripping with sarcasm, "you do take your job seriously."

"I'm the sheriff. It's up to me to keep the peace in Gila Bend."

"You're the sheriff because that's what I want you to be."

Hatch bit his tongue, thinking about those cowboys out yonder busting the bronc.

"So what happened?" asked Sledge.

"Marshal Sam Benteen showed up."

"What's Benteen doing here?" scowled Savage.

"He followed Allison from Yuma. If you ask me, I'd guess he's hoping Allison will lead him to that Wells Fargo gold. Benteen went into the saloon and came out carrying Allison."

"He killed Allison?" asked Sledge.

"No. Just knocked him out cold."

"Good," said Sledge. "'Cause I want to be the one to put Allison six feet under."

Hatch touched his own cheek. "Allison do that to you?"

"Mind your own business."

"You can go, Sheriff," said Savage.

The abrupt dismissal rankled Hatch. He'd had about all the disrespect from others that he could stomach. First there was Sam Benteen. Hatch knew the U.S. Marshal didn't think much of him. And now here was Sledge, talking down to him. Not to mention John Savage. But at least Savage paid for the privilege.

"So that's why you called me all the way out here?" he asked crossly. "So Sledge could find out where Allison is and pay him back for messing up his face?"

"Yours is not to reason why," said Savage. "You come when I call. If you don't like that arrangement, you can go back to riding the line on a broomtail wearing a Slash S brand."

Hatch grimaced. Savage wanted him to be sheriff because any other man would look askance at things Savage—or rather, his hired hands—did sometimes. There had been that time last winter when Slash S riders had burned out the squatters on Dog Creek, killing a man and his wife in the process. Hatch had turned a blind eye. And then there were the times Savage's men had wrecked Dan Tanner's saloon—so often that Tanner had finally given up and pulled freight. Several times an irate Tanner had insisted that Hatch protect his property, but Hatch had known that Savage wanted Tanner put out of business, since he coveted the saloon for himself. Hatch had always managed to make himself scarce every time the Slash S boys rode in all wild-eyed to wreck Tanner's place, as ordered.

"You got no call to talk to me like that, Mr. Savage," complained Hatch.

John Savage laughed. He propped his booted feet up on the corner of the desk, took a cigar from the humidor, and fired up the long nine.

"I'll talk to you how I please. I own you, Hatch. Don't let wearin' that tin star go to your head. Now you better get on back to Gila Bend. Might be a drunk needs to sober up in your jail, or maybe some tumbleweed spooked a citizen's horse and caused it to run off. That's why you're sheriff, you know, to handle situations like that."

"You can leave Allison to me," said Sledge.

"Allison's gone," snapped Hatch, "and if you go after him you might have Marshal Benteen to deal with, Sledge."

Sledge snorted, looking at the badge on Hatch's shirt. "Tin stars don't stop me."

Hatch turned on his heel and left the room. Savage listened for the sound of hooves on hard-pack as the sheriff rode away. Then he glanced at Sledge, who was heading for the great outdoors, too.

"Where are you going?"

"Find Allison."

"You work for me, remember?"

"Maybe I'll have to stop working for you."

Savage pursed his lips. He couldn't push this man around the way he did that gutless Tom Hatch.

"I'll make you a deal," he said. "You go after Allison. But you don't kill him until he takes you to the gold."

"So you want that Wells Fargo shipment for yourself."

"Hell, yes. Doesn't everybody?"

Sledge nodded. "Okay." He continued toward the door.

"Sledge."

He turned.

"You wouldn't cross me, would you?" asked Savage. "I mean, you wouldn't just take off for the tall timber once you got your hands on my gold, would you?"

"*Your* gold?" Sledge smiled. "What if I did? What could you do to stop me?"

With that he was gone.

Savage pondered Sledge's last question.

"Reckon I'd just have to hire somebody meaner and faster than you, Mr. Sledge," he murmured to an empty room.

13

Frank Allison came to when the sun was high and hot in a blistered sky. He opened his eyes and the sunlight lanced painfully into his brain. Groaning, he rolled over. And then the nausea hit him, and the bile rose in his throat, and he vomited. His head pounded with a hangover to end all hangovers.

In time, he recovered sufficiently to sit up and take notice of things around him. The first thing he noticed was Sam Benteen, sitting on his saddle in the shade of a scrawny creosote bush. The marshal was whittling on a stick.

Allison then took note of the ashes of a long-dead fire in a circle of stones. Over there was the dun gelding, tethered to a wind-twisted cypress that had pushed its way up through a pile of big rocks. Then he broadened his horizons, and realized they were camped in a shallow canyon. Buzzards soared on the hot air currents overhead. They figured he was dead. Well, they weren't too far off the mark.

"How do you feel?" asked Benteen.

"I'd have to die to get better."

Benteen nodded sympathetically. "As I recall, you used to could handle the likker. But I guess five years in the hoosegow cured you of that."

"I was lucky sometimes to get water." Allison gingerly touched the side of his head, felt the big knot there. "What did you hit me with?"

"A bottle."

Allison remembered now—remembered sitting in the Antelope Saloon drinking himself into a stupor. Remembered, too, why he had been doing that.

Angie . . .

He succumbed to another wave of stomach-churning nausea. But this time he just dry-heaved. Angry at himself for being in such a wretched condition, he stood up. The ground tilted sharply beneath him, and he staggered. Caught himself and stood there, eyes squeezed shut, legs braced like a sailor's on the rolling deck of a storm-tossed ship.

"Where you going?" asked Benteen.

"What does it matter?"

The marshal grimaced. He'd heard plenty of that kind of talk last night, and had entertained the hope that Allison might be more clearheaded about things today.

"Just thought you might like to go see your daughter."

"She's better off . . . "

"I know, I know. She's better off not knowing who you are. I didn't say she had to know. I just wondered if *you* wanted to see *her*."

"I . . ." Allison paused, and was somewhat surprised to discover that, indeed, he *did* at least want to see what little Sarah looked like. But he was afraid of what it might do to his already broken heart. What if she looked just like her mother? Allison wasn't sure he could handle that. But curiosity was getting the better of him.

"You know where she is?"

"I can find out."

"Why are you doing all this for me, Marshal?"

Benteen kept whittling. He gave the question serious consideration before answering. Finally, he shrugged.

"You're an owlhoot, Frank, but not as bad as most, in my book. The men you killed were all bad *hombres*. You never to my knowledge shot an innocent person, and the shooting you did was in a fair fight, to boot. You weren't half as bad as that Jack Weller. How'd you ever fall in with the likes of him?"

"We were planning to rob the same stagecoach. It was either work together or kill each other."

"You're lucky he didn't backshoot you and take that gold."

"I watched my back. Besides, you were hot on our heels. We didn't have time to have a falling out."

"I want you to go straight, Frank. Purely selfish on my part. If you stay on the owlhoot trail, you and me might end up trading lead someday. I'd rather avoid that, if possible. So I had high hopes for you and Angie."

"So did I," said Allison bitterly.

"Difference is, I haven't given up hope. Angie's dead, but your daughter isn't."

"Forget it."

Benteen nodded, rose, and picked up his saddle. "Okay. Let's ride for Gila Bend."

"There's something else you want," said Allison. "The gold."

"Sure I do. I want it returned to Wells Fargo."

"Weren't for the gold, you wouldn't care if I lived or died."

"That's not true."

"I'll take you to it."

Benteen was startled. "Are you pulling my leg, Frank?"

"No. It's about two days' ride from here. But I'll need a horse."

"I'll get you a horse."

In better spirits, Benteen carried the three-quarters rig over to the dun gelding and slapped it on the horse's back. He was thinking that maybe there was hope for Frank Allison yet.

They rode double into Gila Bend, and stopped off at the livery stable on the edge of town. Benteen bartered with the man who ran the place, a crusty gristleneck named Jackson, for a horse. Jackson liked to haggle more than anything in the world, so it took some time, but they finally agreed on the price of a hundred dollars for a long-legged three-year-old sorrel with a blazed face. Jackson threw in an old hull for free. Benteen told him that he would go to the bank and get a draft. The United States government would buy Allison's horse.

"I'll get it back from Wells Fargo," Benteen told Allison. "That gold you took belonged to the government. Wells Fargo had to make good the loss. So I reckon they'll be happy to trade you a horse for the gold."

Allison accepted the arrangement. He didn't have much choice, with only a few dollars in his pocket. Realized, with dismay, that he had spent most of the twelve dollars Warden Scully had provided him with on liquor. Well, at least he had paid for the who-hit-john.

Benteen told him to stay put at the livery while he went out to discover Sarah's whereabouts.

He was back in an hour—the longest hour of Frank Allison's life.

"You're still here," said the marshal.

"Sound surprised."

"Wasn't sure you wouldn't ride off on your new cayuse."

"It crossed my mind. Did you find her?"

Benteen nodded. "Seems Angie got a friend of hers to promise to look out for Sarah. That was when Angie was real sick. Guess she knew she might not make it."

"Who is this friend?"

"Woman named Bradley. Runs a boarding-house. Her husband's a freighter. They've got a boy of their own, about Sarah's age."

Allison drew a deep breath. "Sounds like a good place for her. Do they . . . know about me?"

"Yeah. Angie told 'em. You still want to see your daughter?"

Allison nodded. "But I don't want to *meet* her, Benteen."

"Figured as much. It's been arranged."

Benteen gave Jackson the bank draft, and he and Allison rode through town to the Bradley house, a two-story Victorian structure of weathered clapboard, complete with some gingerbread—something of an architectural oddity in Gila Bend, where one-story adobe was the norm.

A woman sat in a rocking chair on the porch, knitting a shawl. Her gray-flecked hair was pulled severely back in a bun. Her face was deeply etched by lines of hardship, but there was kindness and compassion there. Two children were playing with marbles on the porch—a boy and a girl. The little girl would squeal with delight every time a rolling marble escaped her, and she would scamper after it. She was clad in a pale yellow dress trimmed in lace, and her golden curls were done up in a ponytail.

Benteen angled his horse over to the white picket fence that encircled the house. Allison reluctantly followed.

"Howdy, Mrs. Bradley," called the marshal, touching the brim of his sweat-stained old campaign hat.

The woman rose from the rocking chair. "Hello, Marshal." She looked curiously at Allison, then glanced at the little girl.

The children were running up to the fence, fascinated as much by the big horses as by the strangers in the saddles. Benteen exchanged a few pleasantries with the Bradley woman. Allison scarcely heard their words. He couldn't take his eyes off little Sarah. She *did* resemble her mother, and seeing her made his heart ache.

"Are you a sheriff?" the boy asked Benteen, spotting the ball-pointed star in its circlet of steel on Benteen's shirt.

"U.S. Marshal, son."

Sarah was looking up at Allison. "Who are you?" she asked, smiling.

Allison glanced at Benteen. The marshal was watching him, inscrutable.

"Nobody," muttered Allison, and was ashamed to realize how literally true that was. "Let's go, Benteen," he said.

He reined his horse sharply and kicked it into a canter. Benteen gave Mrs. Bradley a nod and went after him.

They rode in silence for a spell, stirrup to stirrup, putting Gila Bend behind them, along a wagon trace that wound its way across a flat cut by arroyos and covered with sagebrush and saguaro.

"I'm sure Mrs. Bradley treats Sarah like she's her own blood," remarked Benteen, at length.

"Seems like a decent woman."

"She is that. She'll take good care of your daughter, Frank."

Allison was grimly silent.

14

A few miles out of Gila Bend they heard the distant drumbeat of a horse at the gallop, and looked back to see a lone rider coming up the road. They checked their horses and waited.

It was Rebecca Savage.

She was dressed like a man, in shirt and jeans and hat, and she rode like one, too. Allison made note of the Winchester repeater in a saddle boot.

"You're Frank Allison," she said.

"I told you as much."

"But you're *that* Frank Allison. The gunfighter."

"Wait a minute," said Benteen, perplexed. "What's going on here? Ma'am, just who exactly are you?"

"Rebecca Savage," said Allison.

"John Savage's sister?" queried the marshal.

"That's right," she said. "But I'm not proud of it."

"Shows you have some sense," said Benteen. "How do you know Frank?"

"It's a long story," said Allison.

Rebecca smiled. "You might say I was a damsel in distress, and he tried to rescue me from the dragon."

"Huh?" puzzled the lawman.

"Are you running away again?" Allison asked her.

"I came to warn you. The man at the livery told me the two of you had just left town."

"Warn us?"

"It's Sledge. He's gunning for you."

Allison shrugged. "I'm not surprised. He'll just have to stand in line."

"You don't understand. Tom Hatch told Sledge and my brother all about you. And you, too, Marshal. I listened to what they were saying. John told Sledge to go ahead and kill you, *after* you found the gold. Sledge can't be far behind me."

"We're obliged," said Benteen.

"You better be getting back," suggested Allison.

"I'm not going back," she replied flatly. "I want to go with you."

"Lady, this ride won't be any picnic," said Benteen gruffly. "In fact, it could turn out to be downright dangerous."

Determination etched on her face, Rebecca threw a quick look around to find a suitable target. Then she drew the Winchester out of its scabbard, rolled it one-handed to work the lever action, and brought it to her shoulder, firing immediately, three times in quick succession. Sunlight flashed off brass casings as the empties came spinning out of the receiver. She hit a saguaro a hundred feet away, grouping her shots tightly.

"I can take care of myself," she told Benteen.

"I'll be damned," murmured the marshal, impressed. "Where did you learn to shoot like that?"

"I was born out here. My father was Will Savage. I guess you've heard of him."

"Sure I have."

"He sent me east to a finishing school, but that was after he taught me how to shoot. I may be a woman, Marshal, but I can manage nicely, thank you."

Benteen glanced at Allison and shrugged. Abashed, he didn't know what to say.

Seeing that the lawman was evidently leaving the decision up to Allison, Rebecca turned her attention to the gunfighter.

"I'm not going back," she said, adamantly.

"Let's ride," said Allison.

They made good time that day, and by nightfall reached a *tinaja*—a spring-fed rock pool at the base of a turret butte. They let their horses drink, then led them up a brush-choked draw to a spot among some big rocks, above the pool, where they made camp. It was unwise to linger overnight right near a watering hole. That was asking for trouble, since Apache, owlhoot, mustang, or mountain lion might come calling at any time.

Their dinner consisted of two cans of beans and some corn dodgers, courtesy of Sam Benteen. They dug a hole and built a small fire in it. This outlaw oven kept the throw of firelight to a minimum. Benteen used his clasp knife to cut the tops off the cans, and then placed the cans directly in the fire to heat the beans.

"I'm afraid it's pretty plain fare, ma'am," he apologized.

"Don't worry about me, Marshal. When I was thirteen years old I trailed a herd north to the Colorado goldfields with my father. I kept pestering him until he let me go along. He didn't show me any special favors, either. As a matter of fact, I rode drag most of the way."

"You say he sent you to a school back East?"

Rebecca nodded. "He decided I was too much of a tomboy. Actually, I could ride, shoot, and rope better than my brother ever could. I didn't want to go to school, of course, but when my father made up his mind about something . . . well, that was that. So now I know how to curtsey, and carry on polite conversation over tea."

"Why did you come back out here?"

"Why not? The Slash S is my home. I love it, and missed it terribly while I was away. Besides, it's too *civilized* in the East."

Benteen laughed. "Miss Savage, I must say, you're quite a woman. Don't you think so, Frank?"

Allison stood up. "I'll take the first watch."

Benteen tossed him his Henry repeater. "I'll spell you in a few hours."

Allison disappeared into the darkness without another word, heading higher into the rocks, seeking a vantage point.

After a while, Rebecca said, "I don't think he likes me very much."

"Does it matter?"

Rebecca blushed. "Of course not."

Benteen grinned and let it drop. They watched the dying fire, the silence broken by the lonesome lament of a coyote up on the rimrock.

"It's rather odd," she said suddenly.

"What?"

"The two of you riding together. I mean, you're a lawman, and he's an outlaw."

"He was."

"Yet you're friends."

"I wouldn't go that far." Benteen rolled a smoke.

"I heard Sheriff Hatch say he's killed thirteen men."

Benteen shrugged. "I reckon. But every one of 'em was face to face. Fair fights. Other gunslingers, looking to make a name for themselves. At least they tend to kill each other off. Makes my job a lot easier. But, far as I know, Frank Allison never killed a lawman. Not that he didn't have the chance to, on occasion."

"Then why didn't he?"

Benteen peered out into the darkness, in the direction Allison had gone.

"I don't think he ever really wanted to be riding that owlhoot trail, Miss Savage."

"Then why was he?"

"Frank Allison was a young gunhawk when I first came across him. A smart-mouthed, wild-eyed, swaggering boy, who thought he could earn some respect because he was so all-fired quick on the draw. Just like a passel of wet-behind-the-ears shootists who are out gunning for him now." Benteen thought about Billy Cade, and shook his head. "By the time Frank found out what he was getting into, it was too late."

"His gun is notched. Is he proud of killing those thirteen men?"

"Proud? No, not at all proud. Those are his thirteen tickets to hell. I think he wants to toe the line. But damned if it doesn't seem like life has it in for him."

"What do you mean?"

Benteen told her about the five years in Yuma Prison, the Wells Fargo gold, Angie Russell, and little Sarah. He could tell that Rebecca was deeply moved by the tragic story.

"And now he's taking you to the gold?" she asked.

"That's what he says."

"What will happen then?"

"Then I'm going to make sure he gets the reward."

"Wells Fargo would never give *him* the reward! He stole the gold in the first place."

Benteen took one last drag off the roll-your-own and flicked the spent quirly away.

"Aw, hell, I know that, ma'am. But there's more than one way to skin a cat. I want him to have that money. He's gonna need it. After all, he's got a little girl to take care of."

"But I thought you said he intends to leave her with the Bradleys."

Benteen's craggy face was split with a sly grin. "I'm bettin' he'll change his mind."

"Why are you looking at me like that, Marshal?"

"Oh, I was just wondering why you're coming along with us."

"I can't go back. I don't like the way my brother . . ."

"No, ma'am. I meant the real reason."

"I'm sure I don't . . ."

"Never mind." Benteen rolled up in his blankets, groaning as he stretched old, stiff limbs out on the hard ground. "Good night, Miss Savage. Sweet dreams."

Sheriff Tom Hatch was very relieved to know that
Frank Allison was gone. But he didn't have much
time to relax. For the very evening that Allison,
Benteen, and Rebecca Savage spent at the *tinaja*
twenty miles from Gila Bend, Hatch walked his
evening rounds and heard from the barkeep at
the Antelope and one of Ma Larkin's calico queens
that a man who looked like trouble had been asking around about Allison.

News like that did not make it any easier for
Hatch to digest his dinner. Anyone looking for
Allison was probably a gunslinger, which created
yet another crisis for the sheriff. The last thing he
wanted to do was confront a gunslick looking to
make a name for himself, because sometimes
gunslicks were willing to make their reputations
by plugging a badge-toter.

For that reason, Hatch hastened back to his

office with the intention of loading up his scatter-gun. If worse came to worst, being known as a backshooter was a better fate than becoming buzzard bait.

Hatch was so nervous about the shadows on the street that he failed to notice something that would have saved him a lot of grief. The lamp he'd left burning in the jailhouse had been extinguished. But the Gila Bend sheriff didn't notice—until he was through the door and three steps into his office.

"What the . . . ?"

The door slammed shut.

Hatch whirled. Then the gun barrel caught him at the base of the skull. A white flash blinded him. His knees turned to jelly and he crumpled. A wave of nausea made him puke his dinner all over the floor.

Jack Weller struck a match on the kneehole desk behind which he was sitting and lit the kerosene lamp. That done, he grinned at Lute Springer, very pleased with the way things were going. The serape-clad longrider was standing over the half-conscious Hatch, having plucked the sheriff's six-shooter from his holster.

"Get him up," said Weller.

Springer kicked Hatch in the kidney. The sheriff uttered a shrill cry and writhed in pain.

"Shut your mouth," snarled Springer, and kicked him again.

"No, no, no," said Weller. He got up, walked over to the stove, and picked up the coffeepot. He poured the contents on Hatch's head. Hatch screamed hoarsely and writhed and tried to protect his face with his arms as the hot crank scalded him.

"Better get up," advised Weller, "or I'm going to let Dog have you. Dog!"

The wolf-dog had been sitting in a corner of the room. Now, with a low growl that made Springer's skin crawl, the beast advanced on Hatch, head down and ears back.

With a strangled cry Hatch scrambled to his feet, fetched up against the desk.

"Call him off!" gasped the terrified lawman.

"Dog, stay," snapped Weller.

The wolf-dog sat on its haunches a few feet from Hatch and watched the sheriff's every move.

For the first time, Hatch got a good look at his two assailants. He recognized Weller.

"You!"

Weller chuckled. "Been thumbing through your wanted posters, haven't you, Sheriff?"

"What do you want here?"

"Kind of you to ask. I want Frank Allison, that's what."

Hatch saw a glimmer of hope then. If it was Allison they were after, maybe they weren't going to kill him after all.

"Allison was here, but he's gone."

"Keep talking."

"He and Sam Benteen rode out today."

Springer fired a startled look at Weller. "Marshal Benteen!"

"The gold," muttered Weller.

Hatch nodded. "That's right. They went after the gold."

He didn't know that for a fact, but it made sense—just as disagreeing with Jack Weller *didn't* make sense. Had Weller insisted that the moon was green, Hatch would have concurred wholeheartedly.

"That sonuvabitch," snarled Weller, his face dark with anger. "Allison's giving up the gold." He lunged without warning at Hatch. His hand around the sheriff's throat, he pushed Hatch down across the desk. Drawing his six-gun, he put the barrel to Hatch's forehead, just above the bridge of the nose.

"You better talk straight to me, starpacker," he said. "Where's that woman Allison came here to see?"

"She's . . . she's dead."

"Dead?"

"Swear to God. She died a couple months back."

"Damn," muttered Weller.

"That means Allison has no reason to come back here," said Springer.

"Yes he does," gasped Hatch.

"What for?"

"His daughter."

Weller was startled. "Allison? A daughter?" He let go of Hatch, stepped back, and then barked a sharp and sardonic laugh. "How do you like that? Where is the girl?"

Rubbing his throat, Hatch said, "At . . . at the Bradley place. Big house at the north end of town."

"What are you aiming to do?" Springer asked Weller.

"What do you think?"

"You reckon Allison will give you the gold in return for his daughter, safe and sound."

"I knew you were a smart *hombre*."

Horrified, Hatch realized what he had done.

"Oh, Jesus, no . . ."

He lunged at Weller.

Weller's gun spoke. The bullet smashed the sheriff's knee, spraying blood and bone fragments. Hatch collapsed, his mouth gaping wide in a silent scream.

"Damn it, Jack," snapped Springer. "You'll bring the whole town down on us."

Weller took careful aim and fired again. This time the bullet shattered Hatch's shoulder.

"Nothing I hate worse than a starpacker," he said, and fired a third time. A head shot.

Moving fast, Weller snatched up the kerosene lamp and hurled it against a wall. The chimney shattered in a spray of flame.

"Let's get out of here," he said.

They bolted out of the jailhouse, the wolf-dog on their heels.

"I can't believe you killed a lawman," rasped Springer as he followed Weller through an alley to their horses, which were tethered behind the Gila Bend jail.

"Not much of a lawman," replied Weller. "Besides, we needed a diversion."

Mounting up, they rode through the alley and emerged onto the street. Weller glimpsed the dark shapes of running men heading for the jailhouse, could hear their shouts of puzzled alarm. Grinning, he reined his horse sharply and galloped north, Springer following, and the wolf-dog loping along-side his horse.

Reaching the Bradley house, Weller had no doubt this was the place Hatch had described. A woman was standing on the porch, two children by her side. Weller figured they'd heard the com-motion in town and had stepped out to see what they could see. He told Springer to stay put and dismounted at the gate in the picket fence.

"You Mrs. Bradley?"

"I am. Who are you?"

"Your husband home?"

There was something about Weller that made her uneasy, and she turned suddenly to the chil-dren as Weller came through the gate. "Go inside now, Benjamin, Sarah."

"I wouldn't do that," said Weller.

He drew his gun.

Springer thought, My God he's gonna shoot the woman, and felt the noose tightening around his neck.

But as the children made for the door, Weller fired a shot over their heads. The children ran crying back to the woman, clinging to her skirt, hiding behind her, while she stood straight and stern and seemingly unafraid.

"You're a sorry excuse for a man," she said scornfully as Weller reached the porch steps. "Shooting at little children."

"Just trying to get their attention. I wouldn't

shoot 'em. But I will shoot you if you give me any trouble, lady."

"What do you want?" she asked, chin lifted in defiance.

"The little girl."

"Never," she replied, and launched herself at Weller, yelling at the children to run.

Weller backhanded her, hard, and she sprawled across the steps. The boy, Benjamin, threw himself at his mother's attacker, but Weller knocked him down, too, and snatched up little Sarah before the girl could escape. Too frightened to resist, rigid with fear, she sobbed as Weller tucked her under an arm and turned back to Mrs. Bradley, lying stunned at his feet.

"You tell Frank Allison I'll trade him his daughter for my gold. Tell him to meet me at the old hideout. And he better come alone—or the girl's dead."

With that he returned to his horse. Handing Sarah over to Springer, he remounted.

"Don't drop her, Lute," he said. "She's worth twenty-five thousand dollars."

Laughing, he led the way out of Gila Bend at a gallop.

16

They left the *tinaja* before sunrise and traveled all day across the blistered malpais. Allison was always in the lead, and he made straight for a range of rugged peaks, cobalt-blue in the distance, seeming to float above the heat shimmer. Mile after arduous mile of sagebrush flats they rode, and for all the miles they put behind them, they did not seem to draw any closer to the high country.

Benteen was confident that they were on the right track. It was across this very malpais that he had pursued Jack Weller and Frank Allison after their robbery of the Wells Fargo stage run between Yuma and Fort Kearny. Into the mountains straight ahead the chase had led. At a small village at the base of those peaks he had surprised Weller and almost captured him. Weller had run south for the border. Allison had plunged into the mountains. Aware that Allison had the gold, Benteen of course had gone after him.

Rebecca held up well, noted Benteen. Everything about her impressed hell out of him. She could ride and she could shoot. She was as tough as she was pretty. He decided that had he been twenty years younger and unmarried he would have courted her, in his rough frontier way. But it probably would have been all for naught. Benteen had a gut hunch about Rebecca Savage. She had taken a strong and sudden liking to Allison. That was the way it had happened with him and Carmelita—one look and it was all over.

He knew he was right. Her being here with them didn't make a lick of sense any other way. Knowing that this hired gun named Sledge was on their trail, she would do better to run the other way. Yet here she was, following Allison into what was bound to be all kinds of trouble.

Benteen wasn't as worried about Sledge as he was about Antonio Rigas. Where was Antonio? Hadn't been any sign of him at Gila Bend. But Benteen was sure that was precisely where Antonio had been headed when he gave up his badge and rode out of Yuma. It could only mean that Antonio was lying low, watching, waiting for the right moment to make his move. He was as cunning as a fox, that boy. And he wanted the gold. It was that *bandolero* blood in him. He would show up, all of a sudden like, once they had the gold. Of this Benteen was certain.

Then what? Antonio, for good or bad, was

Carmelita's flesh and blood. The last thing Benteen wanted to do was kill him. How would he explain that when he got home?

So they had two dangerous men to deal with. Sledge and Antonio. Benteen had faced worse odds. The big problem this go-round, though, was Allison. Frank seemed bound and determined to avoid shooting anybody, even to save his own hide. Benteen kept thinking about the confrontation at the ferry just outside Yuma Prison, with the young gunhawk Billy Cade. Benteen had waited until the last instant to shoot Cade, expecting Allison to defend himself. Would Frank really have let Cade gun him down?

As the purple shadows of twilight began to fill the arroyos, they finally arrived at the mountains. Skirting the little village of San Pedro, where Benteen had caught Jack Weller literally with his pants down, they began the long ascent, up through a steep notch between two peaks, along a trail clinging precariously to a mountainside. At places the drop was perpendicular. At others, steep talus slopes descended to the rocky canyon below. In the failing light it was a doubly dangerous passage, but Allison kept on.

The trail brought them to a narrow valley, and here Allison paused to point across the way to the opposite slope.

"The gold's there," he announced.

Benteen scanned the deserted mining camp—a scattering of ramshackle huts below the black gaping maw of the tunnel, a tongue of narrow gauge rail emerging a short distance from the tunnel to the *arrastra*.

The marshal didn't know a whole lot about mining, but he knew enough to identify the *arrastra*, a primitive ore-crushing device. This, then, had been a pretty poor outfit, unable to come up with sufficient capital to purchase stamping machinery like a Blake jaw-crusher. Blake's "jaws" were a set of iron plates that, when brought together by a gear powered by a steam engine, could crush up to a hundred tons of rock a day.

Such sophisticated machinery had been beyond the means of the hardscrabble bunch that had worked this mine. The *arrastra* operated on the same principle as a stamping machine. Instead of iron plates it had heavy, flat-sided boulders encased in a timber frame. The boulders, powered by man or mule, were dragged across chunks of ore. The gold dust was then collected by pouring the pulverized ore into the sluice box. Water was brought to the upper end of the sluice box by the simple expedient of organizing a bucket brigade, which drew its water from the creek that danced across the bottom of the valley.

Problem with the *arrastra* was that it could process only free-milling ore, the kind whose gold was easily separated from the rock, and it could not crush the ore fine enough to extract even half the gold.

Apparently the mine had played out, or perhaps the outfit had reached the limits of its ability to follow the vein into the guts of the mountain.

Whatever the case, the camp had long been abandoned.

"That's where you hid the gold?" asked Benteen.

Allison nodded. "Not far down the main drift there's a shaft. I dropped the bags down there."

"A shaft? How deep?"

Allison smiled. "Don't know. I haven't been back since. If you recall, you caught up with me the next day and hauled me off to Yuma Prison."

"I spent a week looking for that gold all up and down this valley and the canyon back there a ways. I knew you had it when you lit out of San Pedro."

"You didn't look in there, I guess."

"Is there a gallows frame?"

"Yeah."

It was slap dark. Full night. An early moon had risen above the shoulder of a peak.

"Want to wait until morning?" asked Benteen.

"No point in that. It's always night in that shaft. All we need to find is a lantern and enough rope."

They descended a treacherous talus slope, sending a small avalanche of stones rattling down into the creek below. Splashing across the stream, they rode up along the sluice box. Benteen noticed that the box was falling apart.

"How long has this mine been abandoned?" he wondered aloud.

"I heard about it down in San Pedro," said Allison. "Mexicans ran it. There was an accident. They were digging out a cross-cut and there was a cave-in. Five men were buried alive. By the time the others could reach them they were dead. From that time on, they say, the mine was haunted. The spirits of the dead miners wanted the others to stop digging before more lives were lost. Or so the story goes. I guess they finally got the message."

"A haunted mine." Benteen chuckled. "So you figured it was a pretty safe bet nobody would go down into that shaft."

"Nothing's for sure."

Reaching the mouth of the tunnel, they dismounted. Allison handed his reins to Rebecca.

"Reckon you'd better wait out here, ma'am."

"I'd rather not."

"You afraid of ghosts, Miss Savage?" asked Benteen.

"It's the living, not the dead, who frighten me, Marshal."

Allison knew what she meant.

Sledge.

He had a feeling the man wasn't far behind them. A lot of years on the owlhoot trail had given him a kind of sixth sense about that.

They tethered their horses to a rocker lying on its side near the mine entrance. Entering the drift, Benteen flicked a match to life, providing enough light for Allison to locate a lantern on the ground just inside the entrance. Allison shook it and was pleased to hear the slosh of some kerosene in the base. Not much, but it would have to do. Benteen's match burned down to his fingertips, so he dropped it and fired up another, with which he lit the lantern.

Holding the light aloft, Allison led the way

deeper into the mountain. Benteen decided he didn't much like the looks of the support braces. The timber looked none too solid. A loud noise would be enough to bring the mountain down on top of them.

They reached the shaft about a hundred feet from the entrance. Benteen had retrieved a length of rope in the drift, and a search in the vicinity of the shaft turned up some more. Inspecting the rope, Benteen shook his head.

"I wouldn't trust this hard twist, Frank," he said dubiously. "It's almost as old as I am." He held up a frayed end as proof.

"I want to get that gold out of this hole," said Allison, resolute.

Rebecca ventured near the rim of the vertical shaft. Holding onto the gallows frame, she leaned over and looked down into pitch blackness. A stone the size of a man's fist lay near her feet; she kicked it over the edge and counted to three under her breath before she heard the stone strike bottom.

"Pretty deep," she said, apprehensive.

"It's okay," said Allison. "Loan me your knife, Marshal."

Benteen handed over his clasp knife. Allison used it to splice the two lengths of rope together. He calculated that gave him about fifty feet of rope. Hopefully that would be enough.

Tying the rope around his waist, he tossed the other end over the crosstimber of the gallows frame to a waiting Benteen. Then he unbuckled his gunbelt and handed it to Rebecca.

"Please be careful," she said.

He nodded, sat on the edge of the shaft, and glanced at Benteen. "Ready?"

With a good grip on the rope, Benteen said, "If you are."

Allison slid off the edge, turning his body as he did so, and clung for a moment by his finger-tips to the rim, making sure Benteen was braced to take his full weight. When he let go, Benteen winced, his back complaining with daggers of pain, but he stood fast, letting the rope out a little at a time, ignoring the fact that the rough hemp burned the palms of his hands.

He was almost out of rope to hold onto when it went slack.

"I'm at the bottom," called Allison. A moment later he added, "I can't find the gold. Send down the lantern."

Benteen hauled the rope back up, tied the lantern bale to the end of it, and dropped it down to Allison. Before the lantern reached the bottom of the shaft, Allison shouted up to them that he could see the gold.

A few minutes later Benteen had hauled three canvas sacks up out of the shaft. He untied them, lowered the rope back down to Allison. When Allison called that he was ready, Benteen began to haul him back up. It was rough going. The pain in his back almost wrenched a cry from his lips. Rebecca could see he was suffering. She draped Allison's gunbelt over a shoulder and jumped in to help the lawman. Down in the shaft, Allison did his part, too, getting handholds and footholds on the rough stone, hampered by the fact that he was clutching the lantern with one hand.

"The rope is fraying!" warned Rebecca.

Benteen could see that it was so. "Pull harder!" he yelled, and managed to get a grip on the rope below where it was unraveling before it came completely apart. Rebecca rushed to the rim of the shaft, dropped to her knees, and reached down to grab hold of Allison's arm and help pull him out of the pit.

"Thanks," he said.

"Anytime," said Rebecca.

Allison moved to the canvas bags, opened one, and pulled out a handful of gold for Benteen to see. The marshal was sitting on his heels, breathing heavy, a grimace of pain on his craggy, sweat-streaked features as he flexed his shoulders.

"You okay?" asked Allison, concerned.

"Just getting too damned old," growled Benteen, disgusted.

"Well this ought to make you feel better. It's all here, except for a little that Weller spent on whiskey and a woman in San Pedro."

"Now that you found it," said Sledge as he emerged from the blackness of the drift, "you can start saying your prayers, Allison."

He thumbed back the hammer of his six-gun and drew a bead.

17

Rebecca moved quickly to place herself in the line of fire.

"Get out of the way," growled Sledge.

"I will not," she said, defiant. "You'll just have to shoot me. But then, how will you explain that to my brother?"

"Your brother?" Sledge laughed. It was an unpleasant sound. "I don't expect I'll ever see John Savage again."

"But I thought . . . the gold . . ."

"Oh, yeah. The gold. You were listening in on our little talk, weren't you, lady? That's why you run off, to warn your outlaw friend. I figured as much. Wasn't too surprised to see you riding with these two. But I didn't tell your brother what I thought. He's got the whole Slash S outfit looking for you."

Allison was on his feet now. "Get out of the way, ma'am," he said softly.

"Don't move!" snapped Sledge. Allison was partially hidden from his view by Rebecca, but Sledge knew he was unarmed—he had seen Allison hand his gunbelt to her prior to descending into the shaft. He'd seen it all, in fact, having slipped into the mine only moments after they had entered, and lurked in the shadows of the tunnel while Allison descended into the pit to retrieve the gold.

He could see Benteen, too. The marshal hadn't budged. Was still sitting on his heels, with his hands in plain view.

Rebecca ignored Allison's soft-spoken request. She glared fearlessly at Sledge.

"So you're going to take the gold for yourself."

"You're real smart. Why the hell should I give it to your brother? I got as much right to it as anyone. Yessir, real smart, Miss Savage. You know, it'd be a shame if I had to shoot you. 'Cause you're right pretty, too. With that gold, you and me could have a high ol' time. And we could put a lot of miles between us and John Savage, too."

"I'd rather die than go anywhere with you."

The way she said it infuriated him. "I can oblige you," he snarled, and raised the gun.

Allison shoved Rebecca to the ground and hurled Benteen's clasp knife. The knife struck Sledge high in the shoulder. Dumbfounded, Sledge realized he had forgotten about the knife. Belatedly, he fired, but the bullet screamed harmlessly off rock, because Allison had already dropped, throwing himself across Rebecca, trying to shield her with his own body.

Sledge staggered, swung the gun down to try for Allison a second time, but Benteen was rising now, slapping leather, and Sledge turned that way. Their guns roared simultaneously. Sledge's bullet hit the lawman in the thigh. Benteen hit his mark, too. His bullet shattered the bone in Sledge's gun arm at the elbow. Sledge reeled. The six-shooter slipped from useless fingers.

Allison saw Benteen go down. He saw Sledge drop the gun. But even with a blade and a bullet in him, Sledge wasn't finished. He bent to retrieve the pistol with his left hand. Allison scrambled to his feet and lunged, tackling Sledge. They grappled, rolling. Years of busting rock on the prison chain gang had endowed Allison with tremendous upper-body strength. Sledge was pretty strong, too, but with his wounds he was no match for Allison, who got him pinned down. Allison smashed a fist into his face, then another, and another. Blood spewed from Sledge's broken nose and ruined mouth. Allison kept punching until Sledge was unconscious.

Then he heard the double click of a revolver being cocked.

He stopped punching and looked over his shoulder.

Rebecca was standing there, pointing the gun— not at him, but at Sledge. Her features were as pale and hard as alabaster.

"We ought to kill him," she said flatly.

Allison got to his feet, rubbing blood-smeared knuckles. "There's no need for that."

She looked at him in disbelief. "He's too dangerous to let live."

"Give me the gun, Miss Savage."

She hesitated. He held out his hand. She laid the Remington in it. Then all the tension seemed to drain at once out of her, and she swayed, raising a hand to her face. Allison caught her as she fell forward. In his arms, she revived.

"I'm all right," she breathed. "I . . . I just felt a little faint. . . . "

"Being in a gunfight takes some getting used to."

She looked deep into his eyes. They were face to face, and Allison could feel her warm breath on his lips. She was steady on her feet again, and he let go of her, turning quickly away to go to Benteen.

The marshal was trying to get to his feet. Allison saw that his trouser leg was soaked with blood.

"Better let me take a look at that leg, Marshal."

"Later," growled Benteen. "Listen! Let's get the hell out of here."

Allison listened—and for the first time heard the creak of timbers and the rattle of small stones falling. This came from somewhere down the drift in the direction of the mine entrance.

They wasted no time. Each of them grabbed a bag of gold. Allison supported Benteen as best he could, and they hurried along the drift and out into the night. That was about as far as Benteen could go without a rest, so Allison eased him to the ground and turned back toward the mine.

"Where are you going?" asked Benteen.

"Sledge."

"You loco? That tunnel could collapse any minute."

"Don't go," pleaded Rebecca.

"He's still alive."

"Jesus, Frank," breathed Benteen, incredulous. "He tried to kill us all. What's got into you? I'm beginning to think I liked you better before you went to prison. Lord knows you made more sense."

"I told you," said Allison sternly. "I'm through with killing."

And he vanished into the mine.

"Frank!" Rebecca started after him.

"Let him go!" yelled Benteen. "Damn fool. Gonna get himself killed trying to make up for those thirteen notches. . . . "

Accompanied by a sound like thunder, the ground beneath them began to shudder, and a cloud of dust came billowing out of the drift. An anguished cry on her lips, Rebecca rushed forward. Benteen hollered at her to stop and tried to get to his feet to go after her.

Allison stumbled blindly out of the dust.

Rebecca flew to his side. Relieved, Sam Benteen sank back down to the ground. It didn't bother him all that much that Sledge was buried alive inside the mountain. He scanned the moon-silvered flanks

of the valley. What worried him was a gut hunch—
that Antonio Rigas was somewhere close by.

Allison managed to get Benteen to the nearest
shanty. With the setting of the sun, the night up
here in the mountains had gotten cold. Breaking to
pieces a three-legged chair and a rickety table—the
only furnishings in the one-room shack, Allison
built a fire in the fireplace. But there was nothing
he could do about the thin plank walls of the
ramshackle hut, which leaked cold air like a sieve.

Benteen was fading in and out of conscious-
ness. He'd lost a lot of blood and was going into
shock. Rebecca threw all their blankets over him,
while Allison tore away the blood-soaked trouser leg
and examined the bullet wound in the lawman's leg.

"The lead's still in him," he told Rebecca. "I
have no way of digging it out." Benteen's clasp
knife, far as he knew, was still in Sledge's shoulder. And Sledge was buried under tons of rock.

"What can we do?" she asked, alarmed by
Benteen's unhealthy pallor.

"Best I can do is close up the wound and,
with any luck, stop the bleeding. But we've got to
get him down to San Pedro as soon as it's light."

"What if there's no doctor there?"

"Probably isn't. But I can take the bullet out.
And I reckon they'll have a *curandera*."

To cauterize the bullet hole, Allison took six
cartridges from the loops of his gunbelt. Using his
teeth, he managed to separate slug from casing

and poured the gunpowder contained in the brass shells onto a strip of cloth torn from the sleeve of his shirt, which had been ripped in his struggle with Sledge. Rebecca turned her head, unable to watch as he poured the gunpowder into the bullet hole and ignited it with one of Benteen's strike-anywheres. Benteen's body arched and a moan escaped his lips as the powder flared. The stench of burning flesh turned Rebecca's stomach.

But it worked. The bleeding stopped.

Having done all that they could for Benteen, they huddled side by side near the fire. Every now and then Allison fed another stick of wood into the flames, but he did so sparingly, trying to conserve their supply and make it last through the night.

No words passed between them. As the night grew colder, with the wind whistling through the cracks between the planks of the shanty's wall, Allison draped a blanket around her shoulders. She protested—Benteen needed it more than she. But Allison could see that Benteen was holding his own, now that the bleeding had been stopped. In spite of the blanket, she began to shiver, and he put his arm around her. She slept, her head resting on his shoulder. Allison didn't close his eyes all night. He stared moodily into the fire, thinking about Angie—cold in her grave, saddened by the thought, yet confused, too.

Because he found himself very glad that Rebecca Savage was here.

*   *   *

At first light they were on their way.

Benteen was conscious. Though in great pain, he managed to ride. As before, Allison took the lead. The three canvas sacks filled with double eagles were lashed together with a short length of rope and draped over his saddle horn. As they negotiated the trail above the canyon, he led Benteen's horse by its reins. All the marshal had to do was stay in his saddle. Rebecca brought up the rear, watching Benteen anxiously. If he slipped off the dun gelding at the wrong spot he could plummet to his death on the rocks below.

But Benteen managed to hang on.

They came down out of the mountains without mishap. By the time they reached the outskirts of the little village called San Pedro, Benteen was all used up. There was a church at the edge of town. From it emerged a priest, who took one look at the marshal and insisted that he be brought into the *iglesia*.

Benteen could go no further on his own, and the priest called up a couple of men to help Allison carry the burly lawman inside. They laid him out on one of the rough-hewn benches that served as pews. Allison asked for a knife, and a *curandera*. He spoke very good Spanish. One of the *campesinos* loaned him a knife, and Allison went to work extracting the bullet while the priest sent someone to fetch the medicine woman.

A crowd quickly gathered. Allison had some trouble getting the slug out of Benteen's leg. It was deep, and lying close to the bone. Blood splattered the floor of the church. Rebecca couldn't believe that the lawman had any more blood in him. The priest said a prayer. When finally the misshapen piece of lead struck the floor, Allison was spent. Wiping the sweat from his eyes with the back of a bloody hand, he made room for the *curandera*, a wizened old woman who looked to Rebecca just like a witch from a fairy tale. She had a poultice which, when applied to the wound, stopped the bleeding almost immediately. Allison pushed through the crowd to Rebecca, who stood with her back to the wall of the church.

"I think he'll pull through," he told her.

"Thank God."

"He's a pretty tough *hombre*. But even so, it'll be awhile before he can ride."

"What do we do?"

Allison had been posing that very question to himself all day.

"There's a couple of things I *have* to do. First, I want to make sure Benteen and the gold get back to Yuma. And then I have to get my daughter."

"You're not going to leave her with the Bradleys?"

"I can't."

Rebecca smiled. "I'm glad you can't."

Allison was grim. "I don't know what I'll do . . . "

"The marshal said he was going to make sure you got the reward Wells Fargo offered for the return of that gold."

"Wells Fargo will never pay *me* a reward."

"That's what I said. But the marshal seems to think he can arrange it."

Allison thought it over. His first inclination was to refuse the reward. He didn't deserve it. But then he thought about little Sarah. They would need a grubstake, to make a new start somewhere far from here. . . .

He nodded.

"Reckon I'll take it." He looked long and hard at Rebecca. "But to get Sarah I have to go back to Gila Bend."

"Naturally."

"What I'm getting at . . . "

"I know what you're getting at."

"So what are you going to do, Miss Savage?"

"You might as well start calling me Rebecca," she replied, "because I'm going with you."

18

The *alcalde* of San Pedro, an effusively pleasant man, came to see them. He was a big-bellied, spindly legged man who looked quite bizarre in an old-fashioned frock coat of black broadcloth and a badly dented stovepipe hat. The only word in English he knew was "Howdy" and he used it a lot. Rebecca thought him comical, and could scarcely keep from laughing as he bowed to her with a Continental flourish.

He assured Allison that they were welcome in San Pedro and offered them the use of his humble house for as long as they cared to stay. At his orders, Sam Benteen was carried to his house by the simple expedient of four *campesinos* picking up the bench upon which the unconscious lawman was sprawled.

What followed was an odd procession, thought Rebecca. The mayor led the way, followed by the four men transporting Benteen. The *curandera*, a bent-backed old crone mumbling constantly under her breath, trailed after her patient. Rebecca and Allison came next, leading the three horses, and in their wake came thirty or forty people—men, women, and children—and Rebecca decided this had to be just about the entire population of San Pedro.

"What's going on here?" she asked Allison. "Why are we such a big event? They must not get very many visitors."

Allison smiled. "I reckon it's the gold."

"You mean they want to take it?" she asked. "Is there anyone in this whole territory who *doesn't* want that gold?"

"They won't steal it," he replied. "But they'll treat us like royalty in the hopes that we might part with some of it."

And this he proceeded to do at the *alcalde's* house, a rather modest two-room adobe facing the *zócalo*—the square. After Sam Benteen had been deposited gingerly in the *alcalde's* bed, Allison gave him a double eagle. The *alcalde* protested at first, but his eyes lighted up at the sight of the coin. Allison insisted that he accept it as a token of their appreciation for his selfless hospitality. It didn't take a whole lot to persuade him.

Allison also gave the *curandera* a double eagle, and each of the men who had carried Sam Benteen. The crowd gathered at the doorstep of the *alcalde's* adobe gasped with awe and delight at this generosity. But Allison wasn't finished. He gave two

boys each a double eagle to tend to their horses—
after he and Rebecca had retrieved the rifles from
the saddle boots. He explained that he wanted the
horses fed and watered and curried.

The *alcalde* assured him that if there was anything they needed—anything—they need only ask.
Allison replied that some food would be nice, and
then some peace and quiet, as their road had been
a long and arduous one, and they were tired. The
alcalde understood. He shooed the crowd away,
and the people of San Pedro dispersed, every one
of them trying to dream up some way to serve the
gringo and get a double eagle for themselves.

"You just gave away a hundred and sixty dollars," laughed Rebecca.

Allison shrugged. "They're poor people."

"Who will now do anything for you."

"That's not really why I did it."

"I know. I guess Wells Fargo wouldn't begrudge
a hundred and sixty dollars to the poor people of
this village."

"Yes they would."

They went in to check on Benteen. He was
resting comfortably. Rebecca was pleasantly surprised to see a little color in his cheeks. But she
wrinkled her nose at the smell coming from the
curandera's poultice.

"What did she make that of?" she wondered
aloud.

"You don't want to know."

Allison left the bags of gold on the bed beside
Benteen and returned to the other room. The dirt-

floored room had few furnishings—a table with four chairs, and two more chairs over near the fireplace. Nonetheless, Allison figured these were far and away the best accommodations in town.

He sank into one of the chairs near the hearth with an exhausted sigh.

Rebecca took the other chair. Hearing her quiet movements, he forced open heavy-lidded eyes. She was watching him. She always seemed to be watching him. But, oddly enough, he didn't mind.

"Go to sleep," she said. "You got no rest at all last night. I'll wake you if anything happens."

He knew she could be relied upon. Closing his eyes, he dropped immediately off to sleep.

When he awoke it was almost dark outside. Rebecca was standing in the doorway, and from the square he could hear music—guitars strummed, voices raised in song. He got up and walked over to join her, noticing the food on the table—some *tortillas* and *frijoles*—which evidently had been brought while he slept.

"What is it?" he asked.

"It's beautiful."

He looked over her shoulder at the big fire the villagers had built in the middle of the square, near the well. Sitting beneath the trees, the guitar players were singing a ballad. They sang well, in good harmony. Several couples were dancing around the fire.

Rebecca looked at him. Her eyes were bright,

her smile warm. "Is that for us, do you think?"

"Any excuse to have a *fandango*." He got lost in her eyes for a moment, shook himself loose from the spell, and turned quickly away, non-plussed. "How's Benteen?"

"I've looked in on him. He seems to be resting quietly."

Allison went into the other room to check on the lawman for himself. He was surprised to find Benteen awake.

"How do you feel?"

"Fine," growled Benteen. "Except for that damned racket. Where are we?"

"San Pedro."

"What's that infernal smell?"

"A poultice."

"You took the bullet out?"

Allison nodded.

"Don't hardly remember a thing after the mine caved in," admitted Benteen. Then he motioned to the sacks of gold on the bed beside him. "You're serious about making a new start, aren't you? The Frank Allison I used to know would have headed for the tall timber, with the gold."

"I'm serious. I want to go back for Sarah, Marshal."

Benteen was pleasantly surprised. He flashed a healthy grin. "That's a good idea. I told Mrs. Bradley you might."

"You did?"

"I was hoping you'd come to your senses. You'll need some money to make that new start. . . . "

"Rebecca told me what you plan to do about the reward."

"Now don't go gettin' all proud on me, boy. Think about Sarah. Without a grubstake you won't get far."

"I've thought about it. So I reckon I better make sure you and that gold get back to Yuma."

"What about the lady?"

"What about her?"

"I think she's kinda taken to you. How do you feel about her?"

"Good God, Benteen. It's only been a few days since I found out about Angie."

Benteen heaved a deep sigh. "Frank, I reckon Angie was a fine person. She helped you get through those long years in prison. And she's the mother of your child. I know you must feel like having anything to do with Miss Savage would be like betraying Angie's memory, but I hope to God you won't let that keep you from . . . well, from taking what life offers."

"I don't know," muttered Allison. "I'm a little confused. . . ."

"Hell, sure you are. But look at it this way. What would Angie want for you? I can tell you, though I never met the lady. She'd want you to be happy. And she'd want that little girl of yours to have a mother. I have a hunch she'd have liked Rebecca Savage. What do you think?"

Allison nodded, not trusting himself to speak further on the subject.

"Go get your little girl, Frank."

"What about you?"

"Well, much as I hate it, I reckon I'm laid up here, for a few days at least. Time enough for you to get to Gila Bend and back. Then we'll all head on down to Yuma and see about that reward."

"Okay," said Allison, making up his mind. "Rebecca will look after you."

"So it's Rebecca now, is it?" Benteen chuckled. "Maybe I've been speechifyin' for nothing, seeing as how you two are on a first-name basis all of a sudden."

"You know, Benteen, you do talk too much."

Benteen snorted. "You're just lucky I'm already hitched, or I'd be giving you a run for your money with that purty gal."

Shaking his head, a smiling Allison turned for the door. "I'll leave in the morning."

"Frank."

"Yeah?"

"There's something else." Benteen was suddenly very serious.

"I'm listening."

"Antonio Rigas."

"What about him?"

"He used to be one of Sheriff Kyle's deputies. That was while you were up in Yuma Prison."

"Used to be?"

"He gave up his badge the day you got out. I think he's after the gold."

Allison was thinking back to that day at the swing station run by the old gristleneck named McGee.

"Yeah. I saw him."

"When?"

Allison told him.

Benteen grimaced. "I have a feeling he's close by. Just thought you ought to know. He's a wild one, Antonio. And he's got a mean streak a mile wide. Watch yourself."

"What am I supposed to do?"

"Defend yourself, dammit."

"He's your wife's son, Benteen."

"Yeah. But I'll kill him if he tries to take this gold."

"You're a hard man."

"Don't be a fool, Frank. You've got a lot to live for. Use that hogleg if you have to. You've been damned lucky so far, with Billy Cade and Sledge. Don't press your luck."

19

"I'm going to Gila Bend," Allison told Rebecca, "to fetch my daughter."

"I'll go with you."

"No. I want you to stay here. Look after Benteen." Allison smiled. "And watch out. I think he likes you."

Do *you*? Rebecca so wanted to pose that question to Allison, but it died on the tip of her tongue, and she looked away, crestfallen.

But she didn't have to ask, because Allison already knew what she wanted to hear from him. Knew, yet he just couldn't say them. Ill at ease, he started for the door.

"You're not leaving now. . . ."

"Just want to check the horses. An early start in the morning."

"You *are* coming back, aren't you?"

"I'll be back in a few minutes."

"You know what I mean."

He stood there at the door, head bowed, thinking about what to say in response and then, once he had chosen the words, working up the nerve to say them.

"I've killed thirteen men, Rebecca."

"That doesn't matter."

"A gunslinger and an outlaw. That's all I've been. Never tried my hand at anything else. Don't know what I'll do from here on . . . "

"Whatever it is, you'll do fine."

He shook his head. "Long as I'm alive I'll have to keep looking over my shoulder for some young gun who wants to make a name for himself."

"Then you'll need somebody to watch your back. Somebody who's handy with a rifle."

He had to smile at that. "Like you?"

"Can you think of anyone better?"

"No," said Allison, suddenly dead serious. "I can't think of anyone better."

Happiness filled her eyes and touched the corners of her mouth in the sweetest smile Allison had ever seen.

"I'll be back," he said.

He left the *alcalde's* house and crossed the hardpack of the village square, checking the night shadows automatically, but not really as carefully as he should, because the image of Rebecca Savage standing there, so slim and lovely, smiling at him that way, kept intruding on his thoughts.

Skirting the celebration in the square, Allison was accosted by several villagers, including the *alcalde*, who looked like he had imbibed a little too much *aguardiente*. They all wanted to know if there was anything they could do to make his stay in their honored village a more pleasant one. Allison politely brushed them off. The *alcalde* was a little hard to get rid of. Was the *casa* satisfactory? The food? Did the *señor* want any liquor? Yes, yes, and no. Allison lengthened his stride, and finally managed to leave the inebriated mayor of San Pedro behind.

He spotted one of the boys to whom he had delegated the responsibility for the horses, and asked the *muchacho* where the horses were stabled. Across the *zócalo* and down the street, he would see them, in a pen beside the house of his father. Allison said *gracias* and bent his steps that way, and soon left the noise of the festivities behind.

Down the darkened street lined with squalid *chozas* he walked, and near the edge of the village found the enclosure of cedar poles which contained the horses. There was a feed trough, a few scraggly trees. Allison slipped between the poles and approached the blazed-face sorrel. Felt of her back and belly, down her legs, pulled one leg up and ran his hand over the iron shoe. The moon was out and he could see a little, but he relied mostly on touch. The sorrel seemed to be in good condition. No sores or swelling. It had been fed and watered and curried to perfection, just as he had requested. . . .

Someone was running down the street.

Tensed for action, Allison melted into the black shadow near the trunk of one of the trees. Instinctively his hand dropped to the Remington on his hip. He could feel the notches carved deep into the grip.

"*Señor! Señor!*"

It was a *campesino*. Allison recognized him as one of those who had carried Benteen from the church to the *alcalde's* house.

Allison emerged from the nightshade. "What is it?"

"*Señor*, there was a man . . . asking about you and your *compañeros*. . . . "

"Who is he?"

The agitated *peón* shrugged expressively. "He did not tell me his name."

"Anybody else see him?"

"No, I do not think so."

"Where was this man?"

"Down by the creek, *señor*."

"When?"

"Just a little while ago. I ran back to the *zócalo* and asked where you were. They told me you had come this way."

"Did you tell this man where to find me?"

"I told him you were staying in the *alcalde's* house."

"What did he look like?"

"I could not see too good. But he was a young man, I think, and he rode a black horse."

"Mexican?"

"Sí."

Antonio Rigas.

Allison gave the *peón* a gold double eagle, one of several he had pocketed for just such an occasion.

"Gracias," he said, and with long, urgent strides headed for the *alcalde's* house.

When the door opened, Rebecca jumped up out of the chair near the fireplace and turned with a smile on her lips, expecting Allison. But the man who entered was a stranger, a young Mexican in *gringo* garb, with a gun in his hand. She whirled, reaching for the Winchester repeating rifle leaning against the wall near the chair. Her hand was almost upon it when the sound of a hammer being pulled back froze her.

"I will kill you if you touch that rifle, *mujer.*"

Rebecca had no doubt he meant it, and was quite capable of the deed.

"What do you want?"

"Where is Allison? Where is Benteen?"

"You mean, where is the gold."

Antonio stepped closer, a cruel smile on his lips. Rebecca was afraid, terribly afraid of this man, but stood her ground. She braced herself, expecting violence from him. He looked like the type—a person who enjoyed inflicting pain and fear. Violence was coiled up inside of him, waiting to be let loose.

Though she tried to prepare herself, his backhanded blow was delivered so quickly that it caught her full on the cheek and knocked her down. Tasting blood, she refrained from crying out. She wasn't going to give him the satisfaction. He leaned over, grabbed her by the shirt, and pulled, trying to haul her to her feet. The shirt ripped, exposing her milky-white breasts. She began to fight him then, but he caught a flailing arm and lifted her, putting his face very close to hers.

"You want to die, bitch?"

"Antonio!"

Antonio swung her around in front of him, an arm around her neck, using her as a human shield.

But there was no one else in the room.

"Antonio!" hollered Benteen. "I'm in here. So's the gold."

Cautiously Antonio approached the door to the other room, keeping Rebecca in front of him. He paused at the threshold to peer in at Benteen, laid up in the bed, a blanket covering him from the chest down.

He noticed, too, the three sacks of gold on the bed beside the marshal.

"Sorry I can't get up," said Benteen.

"Get rid of the *pistola*."

"What gun?"

Antonio put his own gun to Rebecca's head.

"Do what I say, old man, or I will kill her."

Benteen grimaced. "Old man? You really ought to have more respect for your elders, boy. Not to mention your betters."

"Do as I say!"

Benteen drew the gun from under the blanket and tossed it.

"Brave *hombre*," sneered the lawman. "Hiding behind a woman."

Antonio released her and gave her a shove.

"Get the gold," he told her. "Bring it to me."

Holding the torn shirt in place, Rebecca threw a glance at Benteen.

"Don't look to him!" yelled Antonio. "I have the gun. I give the orders. You do what I tell you to do."

Steely-eyed, Benteen drawled, "Antonio, your mother would be ashamed of you if she could see you now."

"Shut up."

"You're no better than your pa."

Antonio raised the gun and fired.

Allison was a stone's throw away from the *alcalde's* house when he heard the shot.

He broke into a run.

Behind him, in the square, the guitars and the singing stopped. There were shouts of query and alarm from the crowd gathered around the fire.

Allison hit the door running full tilt, splintering the wood.

As he stumbled into the house he caught a glimpse of Antonio whirling in the doorway to the other room. Caught a glimpse of the gun in Antonio's hand, too, and saw the spurt of yellow flame from its barrel as Antonio fired. The shot went wide, but not by much. Allison threw himself to the floor, overturning the table in the center of the room. Antonio fired again. The bullet splintered the table and then furrowed the hardpack floor inches from Allison.

Allison drew the Remington.

In the other room, Rebecca lunged for the gun Benteen had thrown away.

"Give it to me!" rasped the lawman, trying to leave the bed.

But Rebecca kept the gun, aiming it two-handed at Antonio, who was still in the doorway.

"I don't like being called a bitch," she said.

And fired.

The bullet slammed Antonio back against the doorframe, catching him in the shoulder. Snarling at the pain, like a thousand wasps stinging his insides, Antonio turned his gun on her.

Allison rose from behind the table and triggered the Remington.

The bullet struck Antonio squarely in the chest. He pitched forward, dead on his feet.

Numb, Allison approached the body. Rebecca burst through the doorway and into his arms. Seeing the condition of her shirt, Allison felt some better about having killed Antonio Rigas.

"Are you hurt?" he asked.

"No. No, I'm fine," she breathed, clinging to him tightly.

"Well, I'm not," growled Benteen. "Somebody help me up."

In trying to get out of the bed, the lawman had fallen. He lay sprawled on the floor, his legs tangled in the blanket.

Allison reluctantly disengaged himself from Rebecca's embrace and went to him, helping him up and back into the bed.

"You're bleeding again," said Allison.

"To hell with it." Benteen stared bleakly at the corpse of Antonio Rigas. "Is he done for?"

Allison hadn't checked. He didn't need to, having shot to kill.

"Yeah. He's crossed the river. Sorry, Benteen."

"Got no damn reason to be sorry. I'm just glad *I* didn't have to shoot him. Would've been hell to pay back at the home place if I had."

As he spoke, Benteen glanced at the adobe wall behind the bed, at the bullet hole, and wondered why Antonio had intentionally missed him with that first shot.

20

The next morning, Allison rode out of San Pedro before the sun was up and headed across the malpais for Gila Bend. A strange excitement danced within him. He was both exhilarated and terrified by the prospect of seeing his daughter again, introducing himself to her, and taking her under his wing.

But would she want to go with him? After all, he was a total stranger. She seemed to be happy living with the Bradleys. Maybe she would prefer to stay. Such apprehensions made Allison's trip all the longer.

Late in the afternoon, as he drew near Gila Bend, he spotted two riders across the sagebrush flats. They called out to him, and he checked the sorrel to wait for them. They looked like cowboys and appeared friendly enough.

"Howdy, mister," said one of the range riders, smiling amiably. "Where you headed?"

"Town."

"Where you coming from?" asked the other. Allison threw a thumb over his shoulder. "Back there."

"Seen a woman between here and there?"

"A woman?" Allison checked the brand on the cowboys' mustangs.

Slash S.

They were looking for Rebecca.

"You gents looking for a particular woman, or just any?" he asked.

The cowboys exchanged glances. One of them chuckled. "That's mighty amusin', pard."

He drew his gun.

Allison's hand dropped to the Remington—a reflex action—as soon as the Slash S rider made his move. But the cowboy was surprisingly quick, and Allison was caught off guard and so was beaten on the draw. The leather-slapping even caught the other cowboy by surprise.

"What in the blue blazes you think you're doing, Ring?"

"I think we ought to take this one back to Mr. Savage."

"How come?"

"I dunno, exactly. I just don't trust him. Who are you, mister?"

Allison hesitated. They didn't recognize him, obviously, but they would surely recognize his name. And he could not see how it would benefit him for them to know it. In the old days an alias would have rolled off his tongue quick as lightning and smooth as moonshine. But not this time. He was rusty.

"See there?" crowed Ring. "He don't want us to know who he is."

"What's going on here?" asked Allison, hoping to salvage the situation with a display of innocence blended with a good strong dose of indignation. "I haven't done anything."

"Maybe not," said Ring, dubious, "but we'll let the boss decide. What business you got in Gila Bend?"

"Just passing through."

"Yeah? Well, you should have better answers for Mr. Savage, pilgrim. He ain't too happy these days, what with his sister up and disappeared and the sheriff shot full of holes."

"The sheriff?"

"Yeah. Ol' Tom Hatch, God rest his soul. Somebody shot him to pieces a couple nights back, and then tried to burn the whole town down."

"It was just the jail, Ring, and it didn't burn," said the other cowboy.

Ring shrugged. "Hand over your thumbbuster, *amigo*," he told Allison.

Allison reluctantly complied, mentally kicking himself for being so careless as to have gotten into this fix.

Right away Ring noticed the thirteen notches. His eyes widened.

"Christ! You know who we got here, Bob? The one and only Frank Allison."

Bob hadn't drawn his pistol yet—but he did now, and with alacrity.

"You *are* Allison, ain't you?" asked Ring.

"Yeah," sighed Allison.

Gloating, Ring gestured in the direction of Gila Bend, still some miles distant. "After you, Mr. Allison. Don't try anything fancy. You do, we'll curl your toes."

Allison nodded and kicked his horse into motion. The two Slash S riders fell in behind him.

Night had fallen by the time they reached Gila Bend. Allison's Slash S escort directed him to the hotel which, apart from the Bradley house was the town's only two-story structure, constructed of weathered and warped clapboard, with a gallery on two sides. The building stood at the corner of the main thoroughfare and a cross street.

As they passed through the lobby, Allison spotted a familiar face.

It was Hornsby, the writer.

Hornsby was at the counter, in the process of signing in. He gawked at Allison, adjusted the see-betters higher up on his nose, and gawked some more. Allison's expression was inscrutable as he passed by. Now one of the cowboys was in front of him, leading the way up the narrow stairs, with the other range rider bringing up the rear.

Down the second-floor hall they passed, to the very end, where Ring knocked on a door and was answered by John Savage's curt "Come in."

They entered the room.

Savage was sitting in a chair by the open window, smoking a cigar and watching the street. The cool night breeze ruffled the curtains and tore the blue smoke from the long nine into shreds.

"Look what we brought you, boss," gloated Ring. "The one and only Frank Allison."

Savage rose and walked over to Allison, looking him over from head to toe.

"Doesn't look like much," he said. "Where's his gun?"

Ring handed him the Remington.

Savage examined the thirteen notches.

"Would you like a drink, Allison?" He gestured at the bottle of Old Overshoe on a table beside the chair where he had been sitting.

"No thanks."

"I'm a little surprised to see you."

"I wonder why."

Savage smiled. "Did you kill him?"

"Not exactly. He had an accident."

"Fatal accident?"

"Very."

"Hmm. Sledge never struck me as a careless man."

"Only takes one mistake. He's dead. And you can forget about getting your hands on the gold."

"What about my sister?"

Allison figured there was nothing to be gained with further pretense. Because of what happened on the Yuma stage, Savage had made up his mind that Allison knew where Rebecca was, and he wouldn't accept a denial.

"You can forget about her, too."

Savage was silent a moment, thinking, staring at the Remington in his hand, and Allison wondered what his game was.

"Two men rode into town a couple of days ago," said Savage. "They killed Tom Hatch. They tried to burn the jail down."

"So I heard. What's that got to do with me?"

"Then they went to the Bradley place . . . "

Allison's blood froze in his veins.

Savage was watching him, and his expression seemed to please the Slash S owner.

"Those two men took the little girl named Sarah. She's your little girl, isn't she, Allison?"

Allison had to beat back a strong urge to get his hands around this supercilious bastard's neck and strangle the wasted life out of him. But he figured the Slash S cowboys would feel obliged to shoot him, and dead he would be of no help to Sarah.

"You know who those two men are, don't you?" asked Savage.

Allison didn't answer. He had a pretty good idea who one of them was, anyway.

Jack Weller.

He'd heard a few rumors about Weller during his five years' incarceration at Yuma Prison. The general consensus was that Weller spent most of his time south of the Bloody Border. There had even been a story going around that bounty hunters had tracked Weller down and brought him in draped over his bloody saddle. Allison hadn't put much stock in that story. No, he'd always figured Weller was alive—and he knew the man well enough to expect him to be after that gold, even after five years. Weller knew about Angie, too. It made sense he would come to Gila Bend if he wanted to have a final reckoning with his old partner. And if he learned, as he would, that Allison was out with Benteen to collect the gold, then he was the kind who would kidnap Sarah and hold her hostage. It would be Sarah for the gold. Two things scared Allison. He didn't have the gold to trade—and the thought of Sarah in Jack Weller's hands was not a pleasant one.

"Look," said Savage. "I'll make a deal with you. I'll give you enough men to catch those two and get your daughter back. You can't do it alone. In return, I want my sister back."

Allison shook his head. "No deal."

"You bastard. . . . "

"Your sister doesn't want to come back," said Allison. "So you'll just have to figure out some other way to get that feller Cabell's land. And as for the help of your hired hands, my daughter would stand a better chance if I go after those two alone."

Scowling, Savage turned to the window. He stood there, his back to Allison, hands clasped behind his back, his head down, and he said nothing for a full minute.

"So what do you want us to do with him, boss?" asked Ring.

"I could have you killed, Allison," said Savage thickly. "Nobody would care."

Allison felt better now. He knew it was an empty threat. "Two people would. The last two people you'd ever want to have to answer to. Sam Benteen and your sister."

"Let him go," muttered Savage.

"What?" queried Ring in disbelief.

"I said let him go!" yelled Savage. "Are you deaf as well as stupid?"

Allison permitted himself a faint smile. "You never had good enough cards to pull this bluff off, Savage."

"It's not over yet, Allison."

But Allison knew that it was. He turned to Ring and held out his hand. The Slash S cowboy surrendered the Remington, and Allison left the room without another word.

He went downstairs to the desk and asked the clerk for Hornsby's room number. Then back upstairs he ran and kicked in the first door to the left of the stairs without bothering to knock.

Hornsby was in the process of unpacking his valise. He whirled, and the look of horror on his face was a wonder to behold.

Allison started towards him. Hornsby uttered a squeaking noise and backed up, bumping against a table, and finally ending up in a corner of the room, shaking like a leaf in a hurricane, his spectacles akimbo on his nose. He raised his hands in a feeble defense.

"Don't . . . don't kill me!" he shrieked.

Allison reached out and grabbed him by the collar.

"You're coming with me."

"Where? Where are we going?" Hornsby had this terrible image of being dragged out into the desert, shot dead, and left for the vultures and coyotes.

"You want a story, don't you?"

"I know you didn't want me to follow you, Mr. Allison, but I . . . "

"Oh, I'm glad to see you, Hornsby."

"What?"

"I reckon there's going to be a shoot-out. Me and Jack Weller. Two of the meanest *hombres* west of the Mississippi. Think that would sell? I just figured you'd want to be there. . . . "

21

On their way out of town that night, Allison stopped off to see Mrs. Bradley. The ugly bruise on her face angered him. She assured him that she was okay and relayed Weller's message.

"Do you know where Sarah is, Mr. Allison?"

Allison nodded.

"Can you get her back safe and sound?"

"I will."

She looked at him, long and hard, and Allison felt as though she were reading his mind. And what she said next seemed to prove this was so.

"Will you let me know where the two of you go, Mr. Allison? I . . . I would like to write to Sarah from time to time. And perhaps someday," she added sadly, "I will see her again."

"I don't know how to thank you for all you've done, ma'am."

"I am the one who should be grateful, Mr. Allison. Grateful for the opportunity of getting to know little Sarah. She is a very special, delightful child. A precious gift."

"I know that now."

"I only wish my husband were here to go with you."

Allison gestured towards Hornsby.

"I've got all the help I need."

Hornsby smiled weakly.

They rode most of the night. It was an ordeal for the easterner. He kept falling asleep in the saddle, which the livery owner, Jackson, had thrown in with the horse, hired out by Allison with the last of his double eagles.

Allison rode stirrup to stirrup with Hornsby, and every time the dime novelist drifted off Allison reached over and shook him roughly awake. Hornsby eventually began to wonder if the night—and the torment—would ever end. Allison finally called a halt a couple of hours before sunrise. Hornsby knew it wasn't for his sake, but for the horses'. He had difficulty dismounting, his joints were so stiff and sore. This had been the longest horseback ride of his life.

"Get some sleep," advised Allison. "We ride at daybreak."

Hornsby just groaned. Stretching out on the hard, cold, rocky ground, he thought briefly of scorpions and rattlesnakes, but such apprehensions were not sufficiently terrifying to keep him awake.

Allison tied the horses to a wolfberry bush, loosened the cinches, and found a good rock to sit on. There he remained all the rest of the night, gazing out across the desert, wondering if Sarah was still alive.

Because he knew Jack Weller was the kind of man who would kill a defenseless little girl without blinking an eye.

The next day was another ordeal for Hornsby. The heat, the dust, the ride, the aching bones, the burning eyes, the dry throat, the growling empty belly. The hammering sun seemed to drive a steel rod through his skull. It got so bad that Hornsby began to think he would have been better off had Allison shot him dead in that Gila Bend hotel room. That would have been mercifully quick, at least.

None of it seemed to bother Allison, Hornsby noticed with some resentment. The man looked like he could just ride forever through this living hell.

They paused at midday to let the horses breathe. Allison uncorked his canteen. Hornsby licked chapped lips with a swollen tongue—and then stared in stupefaction as Allison poured the water in the crown of his hat and let the horses drink.

"My God!" cried Hornsby in pure anguish. "Have mercy. I'm dying of thirst here."

Allison tossed him the canteen. Hornsby drank

what little water remained—barely enough to wet his whistle.

"We've no more water," he said, his voice shaky with panic as he scanned the malpais, doubting that there was any water within a hundred miles of this godforsaken spot. He was going to die a horrible death. He realized that now.

"We're almost there," said Allison.

"Then what?" asked Hornsby, with trepidation. He didn't really want to know.

"Then you're going to help me get my daughter back."

Hornsby gulped. "I'm . . . I'm really no good with firearms, Mr. Allison. . . . "

"You're going to help me," said Allison, his eyes glittering like polished steel.

"Well, yes, of course." Hornsby adjusted his pince-nez. "Certainly."

Lute Springer stepped out of the shack and scanned the rimrock of the box canyon. Then he looked grimly at Jack Weller, who was sitting on the ground, leaning against the shanty's front wall, a rifle across his knees. The wolf-dog lay in the dust nearby.

"It's hot as hell down here," complained Springer.

"The life you've led, you might as well get used to it."

Springer was not amused. He glanced at the notch, about two hundred yards from the cabin—

the only way in or out of this box canyon. Or so said Weller. Springer sure couldn't see any other way; but then it didn't make much sense that Weller would have used this spot for a hideout when on the dodge if there wasn't a back door, in case the law came knocking on the front.

"You reckon he'll ever come?" he asked.

"He'll come," rasped Weller.

"Then what?"

"Then we kill the sonuvabitch and take the gold. What do you mean, then what?"

"Gettin' edgy, Jack?"

"Shut up."

"I meant, then what do we do with the girl?"

"I don't give a good goddamn," said Weller, getting to his feet. "It's *adiós* for me once I get my hands on that gold."

"You mean your share of it."

"Sure. That's what I mean. As for the girl, you can take her with you, seein' as how you're so fond of her. Or you can leave her here, for all I care."

Springer nodded. He had a good idea of the fate that would befall the little girl—because he knew Weller was lying. Weller planned to keep all the gold for himself—which meant he would have to kill one Lute Springer. That had been his plan all along, undoubtedly. As for the girl, she wouldn't survive, either.

"You better get back inside and watch her," said Weller.

"She's still sleeping."

"*Get back inside and watch her.* She's worth

twenty-five thousand dollars, dammit. I'm going to check on the horses."

Weller stalked away, circling around behind the shack. The wolf-dog got up and followed, growling at Springer in passing.

Springer's smile was by far the coldest thing in that box canyon.

Yeah, you know, don't you, hound, he thought. I'm gonna kill your master before he does the same for me. And I'll have a bullet for you, too.

He went back inside, wishing he had never bought into this business. But that, he decided, was what gold did to a man. Made a fool out of him.

Around back of the shanty, Weller checked the horses in a cursory manner. They were secured to a picket rope near the spring, which bubbled up through the rocks to make a small, scum-covered pool. A prospector had once lived here—Weller knew as much because he had found the man's diggings. Apparently there had been far less gold than there was water in this canyon, because the original occupant had been long gone when Weller had started using this place for a hideout.

He hadn't told Springer about it, but there *was* a back way out of the canyon. You had to crawl through a small cave behind the spring, and then up a steep rock chute to a ledge that would take you the rest of the way out. You had to go on foot, but the advantage was that unless you knew right where to find the escape route, you weren't likely to find it. Weller had stumbled upon it quite by accident, and then only after several days of exploring every square foot of the canyon, looking for an emergency exit.

Problem was, Frank Allison knew about it too.

Weller had a feeling Allison was coming—soon.

He was thinking he had better post Springer back here, just in case, when he heard the clatter of an iron-shod horse passing through the notch.

Returning to the front of the shack, he found Springer in the doorway, watching the lone rider emerge from the blue shadows of the notch.

"Who the hell is that?" muttered Springer. He knew the rider wasn't Allison, not in those duds.

"Get back inside," snapped Weller. "Hold onto the girl."

Springer went back inside.

Weller glowered at Hornsby as the easterner rode right up to the shack.

"Good morning, sir," said Hornsby, with a nervous smile. "I am Jonathan Hornsby, at your service. A writer by profession. I understand it is not proper frontier etiquette to ask a man his name, but I . . . well, are you . . . would you happen to be the notorious Jack Weller?"

Nonplussed, Weller said, "What the hell is going on here?"

"Please hear me out, Mr. Weller. I want to write a story about your exploits on the owlhoot trail. I . . . I could make you quite famous. . . . "

"Dog!" growled Weller, drawing his gun. "The horse . . . "

The wolf-dog sprang forward, going for the throat of Hornsby's horse. The horse reared with a shrill whinny, dislodging its rider. Hornsby somersaulted backwards out of the saddle and landed on his face. Stunned, wheezing because the fall had been knocked the wind out of him, Hornsby looked up, yelped in fright, and rolled desperately to avoid being trampled by the horse, which had shaken the wolf-dog loose and turned to flee through the notch, the snarling hound streaking after it.

Hornsby tried to get up, but Weller kicked him in the side and sent him sprawling. The outlaw loomed over him, aiming the gun at his head. Hornsby froze, petrified with fear.

"I'm gonna ask you this just one time," said Weller. "Where's Frank Allison?"

"I'm right here, Jack."

Weller whirled.

Allison was coming around from behind the shanty.

The Remington was in his hand.

Weller leered. "Hullo, Frank. Long time no see. How was prison?"

Allison stopped at the corner of the shack. "Where's my daughter?"

"Where's the gold?"

"I forgot to bring it."

"Then you're a dead man, you bastard," cried Weller, and fired.

The bullet struck the corner of the shack, spraying splinters of brittle wood. Allison threw himself sideways, hit the ground, and rolled up onto one knee. The Remington spoke. Weller was moving, too, running for the cover of a nearby boulder. Allison's bullet caught him in the leg and knocked him down. Sprawled in the dust, cursing, Weller threw more lead at Allison. A bullet creased Allison's arm just below the shoulder, but he scarcely felt it. The Remington spoke again, and again, and again. Gun thunder bounced off the looming walls of the box canyon.

Hornsby watched in horror as the back of Weller's head suddenly dissolved in a spray of blood and brains and skull fragments.

Springer emerged from the shack. He was carrying little Sarah under one arm like a sack of grain, his six-gun in the other hand. Allison whirled. Seeing Sarah, he held his fire. At that instant he became aware of the wolf-dog coming straight at him. Springer raised the gun.

Allison realized he had only one bullet left.

He turned to take the wolf-dog's onslaught—and didn't shoot.

But Springer did.

His bullet caught the hound in mid-leap. It fell at Allison's feet, writhing in the dust a moment, and then was still.

Allison turned to square off with Springer.

"I never liked that damned dog," muttered the serape-clad outlaw.

Sarah was squirming in his grasp, crying, frightened by the gunfire. Springer put her down.

"There's your pa, girl. Go to him."

Sarah ran to Allison, stopping just shy of him.

She turned her tearstained face up to look at him with wide, quizzical eyes.

"Are you really my daddy?"

A slow smile creased Allison's stern, sun-dark features.

"I sure am," he said.

He glanced at Springer, who had holstered his pistol. Allison nodded, and put away the Remington. Then he swept Sarah up in his arms, held her high over his head, bewitched by the way the sun shone in her yellow hair, richer than all the gold in the world.

Hornsby walked over, shaken but unhurt.

"Thanks," said Allison, from the bottom of his heart.

"Oh, well . . . " Hornsby shrugged, trying to appear nonchalant. "My pleasure." He glanced at Weller's corpse and felt sick. "I think I've gotten all the local color I'll ever need, Mr. Allison."

"Going back East?"

"God, yes."

"I want you to write that story about me."

"What? You do?"

"Yeah. And use some of that literary license with the ending."

Hornsby glanced at Sarah . . . and nodded, comprehending.

"The Life and Death of Frank Allison."

Allison handed him the Remington. "I want you to have this."

"Oh, no, I couldn't. . . . "

"I want you to take it, Hornsby. After your book

comes out, I won't need it. And since you have this gun, everybody will believe that I *am* dead."

He walked on, heading for the notch and the sorrel horse beyond it that would take him and little Sarah back to San Pedro, and Rebecca.

"I'll make believers out of them," said Hornsby softly, staring at the thirteen notches.

ᐦ HarperPaperbacks *By Mail*

**To complete your Zane Grey collection, check off
the titles you're missing and order today!**

- ❑ Arizona Ames (0-06-100171-6)............................. $3.99
- ❑ The Arizona Clan (0-06-100457-X).................... $3.99
- ❑ Betty Zane (0-06-100523-1)............................... $3.99
- ❑ Black Mesa (0-06-100291-7)............................... $3.99
- ❑ Blue Feather and Other Stories (0-06-100581-9)....... $3.99
- ❑ The Border Legion (0-06-100083-3)..................... $3.95
- ❑ Boulder Dam (0-06-100111-2)............................. $3.99
- ❑ The Call of the Canyon (0-06-100342-5)............. $3.99
- ❑ Captives of the Desert (0-06-100292-5).............. $3.99
- ❑ Code of the West (0-06-1001173-2).................... $3.99
- ❑ The Deer Stalker (0-06-100147-3)....................... $3.99
- ❑ Desert Gold (0-06-100454-5)............................... $3.99
- ❑ The Drift Fence (0-06-100455-3)........................ $3.99
- ❑ The Dude Ranger (0-06-100055-8)................... $3.99
- ❑ Fighting Caravans (0-06-100456-1)............... $3.99
- ❑ Forlorn River (0-06-100391-3)............................. $3.99
- ❑ The Fugitive Trail (0-06-100442-1).................... $3.99
- ❑ The Hash Knife Outfit (0-06-100452-9)............ $3.99
- ❑ The Heritage of the Desert (0-06-100451-0)....... $3.99
- ❑ Knights of the Range (0-06-100436-7).............. $3.99
- ❑ The Last Trail (0-06-100583-5)........................... $3.99
- ❑ The Light of Western Stars (0-06-100339-5)....... $3.99
- ❑ The Lone Star Ranger (0-06-100450-2).............. $3.99
- ❑ The Lost Wagon Train (0-06-100064-7).............. $3.99
- ❑ Majesty's Rancho (0-06-100341-7)..................... $3.99
- ❑ The Maverick Queen (0-06-100392-1)................. $3.99
- ❑ The Mysterious Rider (0-06-100132-5)................ $3.99
- ❑ Raiders of Spanish Peaks (0-06-100393-X)........ $3.99
- ❑ The Ranger and Other Stories (0-06-100587-8)... $3.99
- ❑ The Reef Girl (0-06-100498-7)............................ $3.99
- ❑ Riders of the Purple Sage (0-06-100469-3).......... $3.99

❑ Robbers' Roost (0-06-100280-1)........................ $3.99
❑ Shadow on the Trail (0-06-100443-X).................... $3.99
❑ The Shepherd of Guadaloupe (0-06-100500-2)..... $3.99
❑ The Spirit of the Border (0-06-100293-3)............... $3.99
❑ Stairs of Sand (0-06-100468-5)........................... $3.99
❑ Stranger From the Tonto (0-06-100174-0)........... $3.99
❑ Sunset Pass (0-06-100084-1)............................. $3.99
❑ Tappan's Burro (0-06-100588-6)......................... $3.99
❑ 30,000 on the Hoof (0-06-100085-X)................... $3.99
❑ Thunder Mountain (0-06-100216-X)...................... $3.99
❑ The Thundering Herd (0-06-100217-8)................. $3.99
❑ The Trail Driver (0-06-100154-6)......................... $3.99
❑ Twin Sombreros (0-06-100101-5)......................... $3.99
❑ Under the Tonto Rim (0-06-100294-1)................... $3.99
❑ The Vanishing American (0-06-100295-X)............. $3.99
❑ Wanderer of the Wasteland (0-06-100092-2)....... $3.99
❑ West of the Pecos (0-06-100467-7)..................... $3.99
❑ Wilderness Trek (0-06-100260-7)........................ $3.99
❑ Wild Horse Mesa (0-06-100338-7)....................... $3.99
❑ Wildfire (0-06-100081-7).................................... $3.99
❑ Wyoming (0-06-100340-9)................................... $3.99

MAIL TO:
HarperCollins Publishers
P.O. Box 588 Dunmore, PA 18512-0588
OR CALL: (800) 331-3761 (Visa/MasterCard)

For Fastest Service

Visa & MasterCard Holders Call
1-800-331-3761

Subtotal..$_____
Postage and Handling...$ 2.00*
Sales Tax (Add applicable sales tax)...........................$_____
TOTAL:...$_____

*(Order 4 or more titles and postage and handling is free! Orders of less than 4 books, please include $2.00 p/h.
Remit in US funds, do not send cash.)

Name_____

Address_____

_____

City_____ State_____ Zip_____

(Valid only in US & Canada)

Allow up to 6 weeks delivery.
Prices subject to change.   H0805